THE LORD OF THE RINGS

COMPLETE

VISUAL COMPANION

THE
LORD
OF THE
RINGS

COMPLETE
VISUAL COMPANION

JUDE FISHER

HOUGHTON MIFFLIN COMPANY

BOSTON · NEW YORK · 2004

THE RINGS OF POWER

Long ago, in the Second Age of Middle-earth, there were forged nineteen Great Rings, each bestowing long life and magical powers upon the wearer. But Sauron, Dark Lord of Mordor, treacherously wrought a Ruling Ring, mixing its molten gold with his own blood and life force, by which he intended to bring all the other Rings under his own control. Deep inside Mount Doom he forged it, and over it he chanted the Ring-spell that would bring it to life:

> *Three Rings for the Elven-kings under the sky,*
>
> *Seven for the Dwarf-lords in their halls of stone,*
>
> *Nine for Mortal Men doomed to die,*
>
> *One for the Dark Lord on his dark throne*
>
> *In the Land of Mordor where the Shadows lie.*
>
> *One Ring to rule them all, One Ring to find them,*
>
> *One Ring to bring them all and in the darkness bind them*
>
> *In the Land of Mordor where the Shadows lie.*

The three Rings held by the Elves remained untouched by his evil, and the rings of the Dwarves were safely sequestered; but the nine held by the lords of men succumbed to him and those who wore them were ensnared, condemned to walk in the permanent twilight of his Eye, reduced to the state of Ringwraiths.

THE LAST ALLIANCE OF ELVES AND MEN

I n the Second Age of the Sun, Sauron cruelly enslaved the Free Peoples of Middle-earth, and his shadow stretched far over the land. Despair and fear fell across the world until a Last Alliance of Elves and Men, under the leadership of the Elven-king Gil-galad and Elendil, High King of Gondor, was forged in a desperate attempt to break his power.

On the slopes of Mount Doom, their great army drove back the Dark Lord's forces; but there Gil-galad, though as an immortal Elf-lord he was never born to die, perished beneath the heat of Sauron's hand; and Elendil fell, too, breaking beneath him his legendary greatsword, Narsil, which had been forged in the First Age by the Dwarves. His son Isildur, prince of Gondor, took up the shard and with its sharp edge struck from the Dark Lord's hand the finger bearing the One Ring, thus breaking at last his will and power.

"So small a thing . . ."

Then the One Ring should have been destroyed; but Isildur succumbed to its seductive power and refused to cast it away, thinking to use it for the good of his people. He carried it with him always until he fell prey to Orcs at the Gladden Fields, and there, in the great River Anduin, the Ring was once more lost.

In this way the Dark Years of the Second Age of Middle-earth ended, and the Third Age began. For thousands of years since that time, Sauron has concentrated his efforts on rebuilding his armies and on his search for the Ruling Ring. But the Ring would not lie still, and by various means has made a long, strange journey.

"He who commands the Ruling Ring . . . commands all"

1

HOBBITS

In the northwestern corner of Middle-earth lies the peaceful agricultural region known as the Shire. And in that part of the Shire called the West Farthing, beyond the East Road, is found the sleepy village of Hobbiton, a quaint rural settlement inhabited by an ancient, unobtrusive folk, known as hobbits, or "hole-dwellers." For hundreds of years they have made a good living in the rich earth of the Shire, and while the earliest of their number may well have lived in simple holes and tunnels, most now dwell in houses that have been built into the grassy hillsides — houses that are low-lying, rounded, and comfortably appointed, much like the hobbits themselves, who stand barely four feet tall and like to eat as much and as often as they can. Daily hobbit meals include Breakfast, Second Breakfast, Elevenses, Luncheon, Afternoon Tea, and Supper, supplemented with plenty of snacks in between. They are a cheerful, settled, well-ordered, and clannish folk, priding themselves on their plenty, their ancestry, and their good common sense; and are therefore most unadventurous by nature: preferring the prospect of a good smoke of pipe-weed with their feet up in front of the fire at the Green Dragon Inn to gallivanting around the world (with the notable exception of one Bilbo Baggins).

Hobbiton remains as inward-looking and complacent as it has been for generation on generation: a place where hobbit-folk can raise their children in safety, grow vegetables and crops, tend their flower-gardens and their animals, and gather mushrooms for dinner; blissfully ignorant of the dark shadows that even now are encroaching from the east, from Mordor. Although activity on the highways has increased in recent years, and strangers are more frequently seen on the outskirts of the Shire, most hobbits remain determinedly unaware that the peace they enjoy is being fiercely protected by the good offices of the wizard, Gandalf (whom they associate more with fireworks than true wizardry), and the Rangers of the North. For Gandalf, the Shire represents a pocket of charm and innocence in an increasingly tainted world. Good-hearted and generous of spirit, hobbits are a folk worth saving from the horrors of the Dark Lord's rule.

BAG END

Hobbits stand less than four feet tall, and their houses are equally compact and rounded: classic features of hobbit architecture include circular doors and windows, curved walls and beams. Their owners set much store by pleasant furnishings and local craftsmanship, specializing particularly in finely turned and polished wood and in skillful cabinetmaking. Hobbit-holes are devoted to comfort and hospitality, containing as they do well-stocked larders, homey hearths, and a ready welcome. Bilbo Baggins's house — Bag End — is a fine example of the type.

BILBO BAGGINS

"Far too eager and curious for a hobbit, most unnatural..."

Scholar, poet, maker of songs, wearer of fancy brocade waistcoats, teller of stories, and friend to Elves, Bilbo Baggins is one of the most famous and long-lived hobbits in the Shire's history. He is best known, however, as an adventurer, a rare thing among hobbits, following the events he has been recording in his book, *There and Back Again, A Hobbit's Tale*, in which he took part in a heroic, epic quest with Gandalf the wizard and several Dwarves, and came back to Hobbiton with a certain Ring, which he had won in a riddle-contest with the creature known as Sméagol, or Gollum. Many of his neighbors — and some of his relatives — now refer to him as "mad Baggins" as a result of these adventures.

Sixty years after returning from his journey, Bilbo celebrated his eleventy-first birthday and passed all his worldly goods to his young relative Frodo, choosing instead to travel to the Elven refuge of Rivendell, there to complete his great work in tranquillity, and to study Elven lore in the company of Elrond Half-elven.

"The Road goes ever on and on
Down from the door where it began.
Now far ahead the Road has gone
And I must follow, if I can ..."

FRODO BAGGINS

"It is a dangerous business, Frodo, going out of your door …"

Orphaned at a young age, Frodo Baggins was adopted by the hobbit he knows as Uncle Bilbo. Bilbo brought Frodo to live with him at his large house at Bag End, not out of charity, but because he was the only one out of all his many relations to show any spirit. Frodo has grown up into a serious, sensitive, and intelligent lad, fascinated by Bilbo's library and by stories of his exotic travels across Middle-earth. An apt pupil, Frodo has even learned to read and speak a little of the Elvish language, an ability that will earn him the name "Elvellon" or Elf-friend.

However, many of the inhabitants of Hobbiton are rather of the opinion that, since he has spent so much time having his head turned by fanciful tales of Elves and Dwarves and dragons, Frodo is not as practical a hobbit as he should be and barely has the sense "to know a rutabaga from a turnip," as the Shire saying goes.

Despite this, Frodo has wandered far and wide around Hobbiton, exploring the highways and byways of the Shire with his friend Sam Gamgee, and as a result has himself developed something of a taste for travel. Which is as well, since he will be called upon to undertake a long journey.

When Bilbo Baggins decides to leave Hobbiton to spend time among the Elves, he leaves not only the house at Bag End, but also the rest of his possessions, including a certain Ring, to Frodo, who must bear it out of the Shire, and way beyond.

"Even the smallest person can change

the course of the future …"

Although it may look no more than a harmless gold band, the Ring is a heavy burden indeed, with its constant temptations and whisperings of Black Speech, the language of Mordor. It has the power to draw the attention of the Enemy's servants, and is the constant focus of Sauron's seeking Eye. Always the Ring wishes to return to its maker.

Whoever bears it will be in constant danger; for his protection, Frodo will receive from Bilbo an Elvish-made sword known as Sting — a magical weapon that has a blade that glows blue to warn that Orcs are close; and a mailshirt made from a marvellous substance called *mithril*, a metal mined from deep and secret places by the Dwarves. As light as a feather, but as hard as dragon scales, it can be concealed beneath clothing, yet will turn the fiercest blade. It was once given to Bilbo by the Dwarf King, Thorin.

SAMWISE GAMGEE

A gardener, like his father, Hamfast (known as "the Gaffer"), Sam Gamgee has spent his whole life in and around the village of Hobbiton. Although he has explored the neighboring areas of the Shire with his friends, on mushroom-gathering expeditions and vegetable-raiding forays, he has never traveled further afield, even though he has been entranced by Bilbo Baggins's exciting tales. Tending the garden at Bag End, Sam has been treated to many of Bilbo's adventure stories about his journeys to foreign parts, where he encountered the more exotic folk of Middle-earth. Elves, in particular, have taken Sam's fancy.

The barmaid at the Green Dragon Inn, Hobbiton's popular hostelry, has also captured Samwise's fancy. Young Rosie Cotton is one of the prettiest hobbits in the Shire, but unfortunately Sam is too shy to make approaches to her, despite the encouragement and teasing of his friends. Instead, he is happy to sit comfortably with a good smoke of pipe-weed and a flagon of the finest Shire ale and listen to the chatter of others.

Quiet, solid, and dependable, Sam has always been the perfect companion for his friend and master, Frodo Baggins, to whom he is devoted. A hobbit of great heart (and great appetite) Sam refuses to be left behind when Frodo first undertakes his quest, although it is not clear at the outset what skills and qualities he can bring to the quest, for while he may be a practical and loyal lad, he is neither startlingly clever, nor obviously brave, nor yet skilled with a sword.

However, adversity can make heroes of even the most unlikely folk. In Sam's case it may forge stubbornness into iron determination and fierce loyalty into extraordinary courage.

MERIADOC BRANDYBUCK

Meriadoc Brandybuck — to give him his full, and rarely used, proper name — is the son of the Master of Brandybuck, and therefore comes from one of the Shire's most prominent and well-to-do families, but he is better known as Merry, an abbreviation that suits well his cheerful, sunny nature.

A mischievous, lively, and audacious lad, he has long been one of Frodo Baggins's closest friends, one fond of practical jokes, pranks, and getting into scrapes, particularly with his cousin Peregrin Took, more widely known as Pippin.

Like all hobbits, he loves to eat, drink, and have fun: mushroom-hunting, scrumping and purloining cabbages and carrots from the fields of neighboring farmers, like Farmer Maggot, or spending comfortable evenings in the bar of the Green Dragon Inn with a smoke of pipe-weed has till now been the extent of his experience of the world; but try keeping Merry Brandybuck at home

when there's an adventure to be had, especially one that may involve a little danger.

Quite how much danger he is likely to see when joining Frodo on his quest, Merry has no idea, of course, but hobbits are a surprising folk whose finest qualities come to the fore particularly in perilous situations, and a mischievous tendency for tricks and japes may be transformed under pressure into resourcefulness and courage.

Armed with a keen-edged short-sword that he is given by the Ranger known as Strider, Merry is soon to discover the true meaning of the word "adventure."

PIPE-WEED

Both Pippin and Merry have a great and practical interest in one of the Shire's favorite exports: pipe-weed, a fragrant burning-herb that is smoked in long clay and wooden pipes. A common or garden variety of Nicotiana, pipe-weed is lovingly grown in various corners of Middle-earth, but it is generally accepted that the finest strains, including Longbottom Leaf and Old Toby, have long been propagated and developed in the South Farthing of the Shire. The habit of smoking pipe-weed has spread far and wide, from the Shire to the lands of men and beyond: Aragorn, son of Arathorn, shares the hobbits' love of the weed, as do the Istari wizards, Gandalf the Grey and Saruman the White.

PEREGRIN TOOK

"Fool of a Took…"

Peregrin Took — known by everyone as Pippin — is the youngest of the four hobbits in the Fellowship of the Ring. Second cousin to Frodo, and cousin, too, to Merry, he has lived in the Shire for his whole life, and never set foot outside its boundaries.

Merry is his closest friend: the pair are quite inseparable, and are hardly ever seen out of one another's company. For years now they have been a menace to the inhabitants of Hobbiton and its surroundings with their high spirits and practical jokes. Events such as Bilbo Baggins's eleventy-first birthday party, with its abundance of ale and fireworks, afford plenty of opportunities for getting into trouble.

If truth be told, though, Pippin is rarely the instigator in these mishaps, but tends to follow unquestioning Merry's lead. Naive, sweet-natured, and more than a little foolish, Pippin is probably the least prepared of all of Frodo's companions for the danger and the darkness they are to meet on their quest. But hobbits are an adaptable, stout-hearted, and determined folk, and while at the outset Pippin may prove to be rather more of a liability than an asset to the Fellowship, he will soon have the use of a sword and the need to use it in his own defense and that of his friends; and use it he will.

HOBBITS' FEET

Hobbits rarely, if ever, wear shoes or boots, and as a result they have developed feet with thick, leathery soles and furry uppers to keep out the cold.

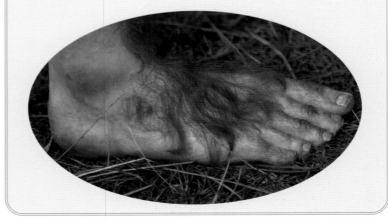

2

MEN

"Men: they are weak. The noble blood of Númenor no longer flows
in their veins. They heed nothing but their own petty desires."

In the Second Age of Middle-earth, Elendil — High King of Gondor — and his son, Isildur, joined forces with the Elves, under the leadership of the legendary Elven-king Gil-galad, to challenge Sauron and the forces of shadow. The Battle of Dagorlad was the bloodiest of conflicts and saw the loss of both Gil-galad and Elendil, but finally the Dark Lord was driven all the way back to the slopes of Mount Doom, and there men and Elves, fighting together for the last time, brought about his fall.

With the broken blade of his father's great-sword, Narsil, Isildur — now himself the High King of men — cut from Sauron's hand the Ruling Ring, which severed him from his supernatural power; and thus the Second Age came to an end.

"There is weakness, there is frailty;
but there is courage also, and honor
to be found in men."

Then should the Dark Lord have been laid low for all time. But men are by their very nature flawed. Instead of destroying the One Ring, Isildur desperately coveted it and decided to keep it for his own use and for the good of his kingdom, declaring that it should henceforth be the heirloom of Gondor and that all those of his bloodline should be bound to its fate. And so it is that three thousand years later, in the Third Age of Middle-earth, his descendant Aragorn, son of Arathorn, last chief of the Dúnedain and heir to the Gondorian kingdom, is to find his own destiny tied to the fate of the Ring and the quest to destroy it.

Isildur fell to an attack of Orcs at the Gladden Fields, and the Ring was lost into the waters of the Anduin. With his death, the race of men was left kingless, and since that time has dwindled and split into different factions and tribes: the Easterlings and Haradrim now support the Dark Lord; the Rohirrim, who dwell in the grasslands and mountains bordering Fangorn Forest, and the Gondorians, whose capital is the White City of Minas Tirith, closest of all kingdoms to the shadow of Mordor. Never, since the fall of Isildur, have the people of Gondor taken another king.

"The blood of Númenor is all but spent,
its pride and dignity forgotten.
Men are scattered, divided, leaderless ..."

BREE

On the eastern border of the Shire, at the crossing of the Great East Road and the North Road, is the town of Bree. This cluster of two-storied, half-timbered stone houses lies nestled against a low wooded hill, and is the home to a motley collection of folk, its inhabitants encompassing both men and hobbits, and even one or two Dwarves. Even more folk enter the town, because of its location at the meeting of two great roads. Because of this strategic position Bree is surrounded by a thick hedge; and a great gate, manned by a gatekeeper, guards each entrance and exit of the Great East Road.

The favorite meeting place in the town is the famous Prancing Pony Inn, the area's most ancient public house, where travelers stop for lodgings and refreshment to break their journeys, and exchange news and gossip from all over Middle-earth. The innkeeper is one Barliman Butterbur, who serves a fine pint of ale, but unfortunately has a less than fine memory.

ARAGORN

"One of them Rangers. Dangerous folk, they are, wandering the Wilds ..."

A tall, weather-beaten man with watchful eyes, well-armed and wrapped in travel-stained clothes, is encountered by the hobbits in the Prancing Pony, the inn at Bree. Barliman Butterbur, the innkeeper, informs them that the man is called Strider, and that he is a Ranger — one of the wandering Northern men — who walk about on their long shanks, turning up from time to time, when folk least expect to see them.

Strider has a dark and dangerous look to him, but he is far more than he at first appears. In evil times, disguise and subterfuge are necessary to ward off the Enemy's eye, and Strider is soon revealed to be a close ally of Gandalf the Grey, and more besides...

The mysterious Strider has the noblest of heritages, for his true name is Aragorn, son of Arathorn, and he is Chief of the Dúnedain, the last remnant in the North of the ancient race of men; and although yet he wears no crown, he is a descendant of the High Kings, the heir to Isildur of Gondor. As a token of his heritage, he bears two ancient and powerful heirlooms: the broken hilt of Narsil, with which Isildur cut the One Ring from Sauron's hand; and the Ring of Barahir, a ring fashioned in the form of twin serpents with emeralds for eyes, their heads meeting beneath golden flowers that one devours and the other upholds.

Orphaned as a child, Aragorn has been raised in the house of Elrond Half-elven in Rivendell, and has long loved Elrond's daughter, the beautiful Arwen Evenstar; but she is of the long-lived Elven race, and he a mortal man, and their future together requires that a terrible choice be made.

Destiny weighs heavily upon Aragorn. As a member of the Fellowship of the Ring, pledged to the service of the Ringbearer, a long quest and a great war lie ahead of him, upon which the future of the Free Peoples of Middle-earth depends. Aragorn, son of Arathorn, has a crucial and unenviable duty to fulfill in both before he can even begin to consider his own concerns.

BOROMIR

"Gondor has no king, Gondor does not need a king ..."

Boromir is the eldest son of Denethor, the current Steward of Gondor, who holds the high-seat of Minas Tirith, the capital city of Gondor. Since the fall of Isildur, son of Elendil, at the Gladden Fields, the Gondorians have taken no king, instead appointing a noble steward to govern the country until the day when the legendary Heir of Isildur may return to claim his throne. Indeed, they have been kingless for so long now that there is no longer any expectation that such a man may exist.

"In a dream I saw the eastern sky grow dark, but in the west, a pale light lingered.

A voice was crying:'Your doom is at hand: Isildur's Bane is found!'"

Boromir has traveled north to Rivendell to seek the meaning of a recurrent dream which told of the waking of "Isildur's Bane" — the thing that caused the High King's death. He will learn in Rivendell that this is the One Ring, now in the possession of Frodo Baggins. Gondor lies closest of all the kingdoms of Middle-earth to the shadow: the dark peaks of Mordor are clearly visible from the battlements of Minas Tirith; and Gondorian warriors have perpetually had to fight off incursions of Orcs and other of the Dark Lord's fell creatures.

Like the ancient High King, Isildur, Boromir can also see a use for the One Ring in the defense of his people; yet when the dark, dishevelled man known as Strider is revealed in Rivendell to be Aragorn, son of Arathorn, last chief of the Dúnedain and heir to the Gondorian kingdom,

Boromir is not fully convinced that he is indeed the man destined to reunite the ancient kingdoms and lead them into a new age.

Despite all his doubts, he still offers his services to the Ringbearer to aid him in his quest, and becomes a valiant member of the Fellowship of the Ring.

Boromir bears with him a great sword, his shield, and the horn of a wild ox, bound with silver and inscribed with ancient letters. It is told that if this horn is blown in dire need anywhere within the boundaries of Gondor, help shall at once be sent to he who blows it; but when Boromir is hard-pressed by Orcs, as the Fellowship travels south, he may be too far beyond the bounds of his homeland for help to arrive in time.

3

ELVES

"They live in both worlds at once — the Seen and the Unseen"

The fairest and oldest of all the races of Middle-earth, the Elves are possessed of great magic and the ability to create things of immense beauty, craft, and enchantment — including the Rings of Power, weaponry, music, language, and lore. Immortal and ageless, they have lived in Middle-earth since the earliest days and were the first of the speaking peoples of the world. But now in the Third Age a great sadness has come upon them, for their time in the world is coming to an end. Elves are now rarely seen in Middle-earth, for many of their number have already passed over the Sea to the Undying Lands, where they may continue to live forever in bliss, away from the cares and trials of a war-torn world.

"Young and old at the same time … so alive, but so sad"

Yet small communities of Elves still survive in the world: in Northern Mirkwood, the great greenwood; at Rivendell, their ancient refuge; and in Lothlórien, the Golden Wood that is the province of the Lady Galadriel and Lord Celeborn. Tall and slender, keen of eye, and mellifluous of speech, Elves have always walked lightly upon the earth. Their songs echo down the ages.

Nai tiruvantel ar varyuvantel i Valar tielyanna nu vilya

May the Valar protect you on your path under the sky

RIVENDELL

"There's magic here, right down deep, where you can't lay your hands on it"

Rivendell has stood for thousands of years as a last haven and hidden refuge protected against all evil things by the power of the Elves. It lies in a deeply riven valley in eastern Eriador, in the foothills of the towering, snow-capped Misty Mountains. There, within sunlit gardens, terraces, and courtyards, nestles a cluster of elegant Elven buildings, ornately carved and decorated with statues, wall-paintings, and fine tapestries.

Its Master is Elrond, lord amongst Elves, and it is in Rivendell that the Council of Elrond is held to discuss the matter of the One Ring and how it may be destroyed.

ELROND

It was during the war against Sauron in the Second Age that Elrond founded the haven of Rivendell as a safe refuge for his people, and he has been its lord ever since that time. He fought in the Battle of Dagorlad in the Last Alliance of Elves and Men, serving as herald to the Elven-king Gil-galad, who fell in that great battle. When Isildur cut the One Ring from Sauron's hand, it was Elrond who urged him to destroy the Ring in the Cracks of Doom, but his wisdom went unheeded, and instead of being destroyed for all time, Sauron was given yet another chance to rebuild his powers.

Millennia old, Elrond Half-elven is the son of Eärendil the Mariner and Elwing. He is a legendary healer and the guardian of a vast store of Elven lore. He is also the bearer of Vilya, the Ring of Air, one of the three great Elven rings that were forged in the Second Age of Middle-earth. His name — Half-elven — derives from his ancestry, for he can trace his line directly back to the hero Beren — a mortal man — and Lúthien, the Elven princess who, out of her great love for Beren, gave up her immortality to live out her days with him in Middle-earth, instead of taking passage to the Undying Lands.

It is Elrond who calls for a Council at Rivendell between representatives of all the Free Peoples of Middle-earth to decide what is to be done with Sauron's Ruling Ring.

Elrond Half-elven's daughter is the beautiful Arwen; and he also raised the heir of the Dúnedain — Aragorn, son of Arathorn — under his protection at the Elven refuge, against the day when Aragorn might claim his rightful inheritance.

ARWEN

Daughter to Elrond, and grand-daughter to Galadriel, Lady of the Golden Wood, Arwen is famed as the most beautiful of all living things. Her hair is dark as a river at night, her eyes of an unearthly blue. She is millennia old and, like her father, is filled with the wisdom of the ages and the lore of the Elves; yet she loves a mortal man. She was raised by the Elves of Lothlórien, the Golden Wood, but when she returned to her father's domain, she there met and fell in love with Aragorn, son of Arathorn, whom Elrond had raised since a boy, following the loss of Aragorn's parents. Now she will be faced with a terrible choice: to act according to Aragorn's will and leave with the other Elves to pass over the Sea into the Undying Lands; or, like her ancestress Lúthien, to give up her deathless future and become his mortal wife.

"The light of the Evenstar does not wax
and wane: it is constant, even in the
greatest darkness"

Arwen wears the great and magical Elven jewel called the Evenstar (a name by which she is also often known). It symbolizes not only her goodness and beauty, but also her longevity; so in giving it to Aragorn to wear on his great journey into shadow, she gives him also her heart, and her life.

"I will bind myself to you, Aragorn of the Dúnedain:
for you I will forsake the immortal life of my people."

LEGOLAS

Prince Legolas — whose name in Elvish means "Greenleaf" — is the son of King Thranduil of the Woodland Realm. He has traveled south to Elrond's Council at Rivendell to act as the envoy of the Woodland Elves who inhabit the great northern forest of Mirkwood. This once-beautiful forest is even now being overrun by Orcs, wolves, and other dark, wandering spirits in thrall to the powers of darkness as the shadow of Mordor stretches ever further across Middle-earth.

The Elves being a long-lived race, Legolas knows the Ranger, Strider, of old and is well aware of his true identity. Like many of his people, he has a distrust of Dwarves, which will result in a prickly relationship with the envoy of the Dwarves of Erebor, Gimli, son of Glóin.

Legolas brings a number of unique and beneficial skills to the Fellowship of the Ring — the brotherhood of Nine Walkers chosen by Elrond to bear the Ring across Middle-earth. Elves have the preternatural ability to move more lightly across the ground than the other peoples of Middle-earth: Legolas is able to run swiftly and effortlessly across the roughest terrain, barely leaving footprints even upon new-fallen snow. As a forest Elf, he is a master of woodcraft, able to scan his environment in order to read even the most minute traces and tracks left by the birds and beasts of the world. He can also see with greater clarity and over longer distances than the rest of the Nine Walkers, and is a superb and deadly shot with an Elvish longbow, which he pledges in Frodo Baggins's service.

Legolas also carries two Elf-knives: long white knives with filigreed blades — deadly weapons, for the Elves make the keenest of all blades in Middle-earth.

LOTHLÓRIEN

"The strange magic of the Golden Wood . . ."

Just east of the Misty Mountains, beside the Silverlode, which flows into the Great River Anduin, lies Lothlórien — the Golden Wood — the fairest Elf-kingdom remaining in Middle-earth.

Lothlórien is home to the Wood Elves, who are almost invisible to visitors to the wood they guard, as they move swiftly and silently through the tree canopy, camouflaged by their magical gray cloaks. Throughout the Golden Wood grow the towering mallorn trees, the tallest and most beautiful trees in Middle-earth.

In the grass of the forest floor bloom the golden stars of elanor and pale white flowers of the niphredil. The silver pillars of the mallorns tower up into a splendid canopy of golden leaves, in the many-leveled branches of which the Elves build their flets: their dwellings, or high houses.

"The heart of Elvendom on Earth . . ."

At the heart of the Golden Wood lies Caras Galadhon, the city in which the Lord Celeborn and Lady Galadriel have their royal hall, a magnificent flet, nestled high in the crown of the mightiest mallorn of all.

THE LADY GALADRIEL

The Lady Galadriel — "lady of light" — grandmother of the Lady Arwen, is an Elven queen of extraordinary beauty, with her timeless features and golden river of hair. She is, however, no mere fey being, but a lady of great power. She bears one of the Great Rings — Nenya, the Ring of Adamant, and with the One Ring in her grasp as well, she would be a mighty match for the Dark Lord Sauron.

"The mirror shows many things — things that were, things that are

and things that might not yet have come to pass"

Galadriel also possesses a magical mirror in which those invited to look may see images of the past, present, or future when determining a course of action.

Her husband is the Lord Celeborn, who comes originally from the northern kingdom of Mirkwood. His hair is long and silver, and his face grave and handsome, showing little sign of his great age.

Lord Celeborn and Lady Galadriel have kept the Golden Wood as a safe haven for those Elves who have chosen to remain in Middle-earth, rather than taking a ship to the Undying Lands, through magical means, and by the vigilant care of their warriors, led by such captains as the Wood-Elf, Haldir.

Galadriel and Celeborn make many wondrous gifts to the Fellowship, including Elven cloaks, which will make them all but invisible to the eyes of their enemies, fastened by brooches fashioned like leaves in silver and green; wafers of lembas, Elvish waybread: though apparently insubstantial, a single bite will sustain a full-grown man; three Elven boats, so that they may make passage down the River Anduin rather than through Orc-ridden lands; an ornate Elvish hunting-knife to Aragorn; a longbow and an exquisitely tooled quiver of arrows to Legolas; silver belts and small silver daggers to Merry and Pippin; a coil of rope made from magical *hithlain* to Sam, which may serve him better than any sword; and for Frodo a crystal phial containing the light of the legendary Eärendil, which will light the darkest places when all other lights go out.

4

DWARVES

One of the most ancient and long-lived of the Free Peoples of Middle-earth are the Dwarves, a tough, stout folk who stand shorter than men but taller than hobbits, and inhabit the hidden places of the world in huge underground cave-systems and tunnel-complexes.

Dwarves are famed for their great prowess in battle, and for their legendary skills in mining and working with both metal and stone. From time immemorial they have crafted extraordinary artifacts in their smithies: the finest of axes, swords, and jewelry; and have created monumental architecture far beneath the earth. Mining deep into the roots of the mountains to extract precious metals and jewels, they came upon the marvelous substance known as mithril — a beautiful silver metal that runs in deep veins through the vast, majestic Dwarven kingdom of Moria, or the Black Chasm, which is called in their language Khazad-dûm. Mithril has remarkable properties, being both incredibly hard and amazingly light, and is therefore highly prized. The Dwarves' love of such riches has gained them a reputation, fairly or unfairly, for gold-hunger and greed.

Following the war between Sauron and the Elves in the Second Age, the Dwarves of Moria retreated from the conflict into their mountain kingdom and closed their doors on the world, so where before there was trade and friendship between the Elves and the Dwarves, there has since been mistrust and even hostility between the two races.

GIMLI

"I've known him since he was knee-high to a hobbit"

One of the noble Dwarves of Erebor, the Lonely Mountain, Gimli, son of Glóin, has been sent as an envoy to the Council of Elrond in Rivendell, where he is to represent his people in the matter of the Ring. There he will volunteer to be one of the Nine Walkers to accompany Frodo on his quest.

Like all Dwarves, Gimli is both stubborn and tough, proud and indomitable, and a mighty warrior. He can also be bad-tempered and cantankerous, and like many of his kin has a deep-seated mistrust of Elves and their strange and sorcerous ways.

Nevertheless, he will pledge his axe in Frodo's service, and even try to bear with reasonably good grace the company of an Elf among the Fellowship.

As befits a great warrior, Gimli wears full armor — a heavy mailshirt, leather armor, and an ornate Dwarvish helmet. He also carries a number of weapons: a tall walking-axe of Ereborian design, with its crescent-mooned blade; two throwing-axes — one a smaller version of the walking-axe, the other a hatchet; and in Khazad-dûm, he will avail himself of a mighty double-headed battle-axe, the epitome of traditional Morian design, as denoted by its powerful, straight, and blocky blades.

MORIA

"Their own masters cannot find them if their secret is forgotten …"

In order to enter the underground Dwarven kingdom of Moria from the old Elven road from Hollin, it is necessary to locate and open one of the invisible gates in the rock. In older times, such doors stood open and were guarded by a doorwarden, but in the Third Age, such days of trust have long passed. If one who knows the secret passes his hands over the rock, pale silver patterns will be revealed, patterns that will glimmer in the light of the Moon: such sigils as the emblems of Durin, Lord of Moria (a hammer and anvil); a crown and seven stars, two trees surmounted by crescent moons, and a single star (the Star of the House of Fëanor) will all shine out.

These symbols have been made of *ithildin* (Elvish for "starmoon"), a substance that mirrors only moonlight and starlight and will disclose itself solely to someone who can speak the ancient languages of Middle-earth.

The inscription on the door is written in an old form of Elvish, and reads: "The Doors of Durin, Lord of Moria. Speak, friend, and enter."

MITHRIL SILVER

"The wealth of Moria was not in gold or jewels, but mithril ..."

Only in the deepest mines of Moria, in the roots of the mountains, was this precious substance found. Other names for it are Moria-silver and true-silver. Its Elvish name is mithril. It was prized more highly than gold, and from it the Dwarves made a metal that was remarkably hard, yet wondrously light. Frodo has inherited a mail-shirt of mithril silver from Bilbo, which had been a gift from the Dwarf King Thorin.

THE ISTARI

T he word "Istari" is an Elvish term denoting an order or brotherhood of wizards.

Such wizards are Maiar — spirits older than Middle-earth itself — who have been sent by the Valar, the oldest and greatest beings of all — out of the Undying Lands into the mortal world to guide the Free Peoples of Middle-earth in their fight against the growing evil of the Dark Lord, Sauron. They have come secretly, limited to the forms of men and to those powers found only within Middle-earth. They may be known by their tall hats, long robes, and by the strange staffs they carry.

Each of the Istari is distinguished by a specific color, denoting their power and rank in the order: thus Saruman, highest of the Istari, is known as "the White" and wears flowing white robes, while Gandalf the Grey begins his journey through Middle-earth as a wizard of lesser power.

GANDALF THE GREY

"It's that wandering conjuror, Gandalf..."

Being fond of the race of hobbits, the wizard Gandalf visits Hobbiton from time to time, to see his friend Bilbo Baggins (with whom he has shared many adventures) and to oversee the safety of the Shire and ensure the shadow that stretches ever further from Mordor does not encroach upon this delightfully sleepy rural backwater.

But to the inhabitants of Hobbiton he is known largely as a wandering conjuror, a blower of smoke-rings, and purveyor of fireworks. Little do the small folk realize the true powers of their occasional visitor. They see only his outward form: that of an old graybeard robed in a dusty cloak with a tall, pointed hat upon his head, a man worn by the passage of time, who uses his staff as a mere walking stick, to lean upon and aid his travel.

"Why did the Valar send me here in this old man's body,

prone to every mortal ache and pain?"

As one of the Istari, Gandalf is able to wield potent magic, and is immensely knowledgeable about Middle-earth's history and the lore of its many peoples. His true age is unknown.

It is Gandalf the Grey, known by the Elves as Mithrandir, who will lead the Fellowship out of Rivendell at the beginning of their quest to destroy the Ruling Ring in the fires of Mount Doom, although the temptation to use the Ring himself must surely be strong. Even though his instinct would be to use it to good purpose, Gandalf knows that the power of the Ring added to his own innate strength would create a force too great and terrible to imagine.

To do battle with the forces of darkness, Gandalf the Grey can call upon not only his spellcraft, but also his staff of power, and the Elven sword, Glamdring.

"It is not the strength of the body that matters,

but the strength of the spirit."

SARUMAN THE WHITE

"The wisest of my Order: his knowledge of Ring-lore is deep.

Long has he studied the arts of the Enemy"

The wizard Saruman the White, Lord of Isengard, is the greatest of the Istari brotherhood, known throughout Middle-earth for his vast store of knowledge of all things arcane and esoteric. He has devoted much study to the matter of the Rings of Power and in particular to the Ruling Ring — its making and its history as it has passed from one hand to another, and into obscurity — believing that if he and his Order find it, they themselves can make the best use of it against the growing power of the Dark Lord.

"The world is changed, Gandalf. A new age is at hand: the Age of Men,

which we must rule. Are we not the Istari? Within this frail human

form does not the spirit of a Maia live?"

Saruman's home is Orthanc, a vast tower hewn from a solid pillar of unbreakable black obsidian that rises to a great pronged spire. The Tower of Orthanc stands at the heart of Isengard, the strategic fortress that lies in a commanding position between the Misty Mountains and the Gap of Rohan. Its main defense is a natural ringwall of stone that measures a mile or more from rim to rim, enclosing beautiful trees and gardens, watered by streams that flow down from the mountains. Unknown to all but Saruman, Isengard is home to one of the rare seeing-stones, the palantír, a great ball of black stone with which the wizard is able to spy upon the whereabouts and fortunes of both allies and foes throughout Middle-earth.

"Creation is the greatest power"

The caverns below Isengard hide another secret. Down there, a new breed of creature is being hatched, as Saruman plans to form an army of his own to rival the Dark Lord's...

THE DARK POWERS

"The Enemy has many spies in his service, many ways of hearing ...
even birds and beasts ..."

Since his fall at the Battle of Dagorlad, Sauron has been regrouping his forces, even though he has failed to find again the Ruling Ring that he so treacherously forged and that was taken from him by Isildur, the High-king of Gondor, and then lost, seemingly forever.

In the millennia that have passed since his fall he has slowly but inexorably increased his great army of fell beings and rebuilt his fortress at Barad-dûr. His powers are now so strong that if he can lay his hands upon the One Ring once more he will be able to break down all resistance in Middle-earth and cover all the lands in a second darkness.

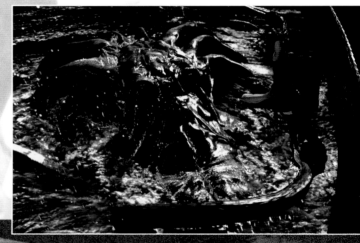

His Eye ever seeks his Ruling Ring, and he has many servants upon whom to call as his spies and soldiery. The greatest and most fearsome of these are his Nazgûl, known also as the Ringwraiths; but the forces of darkness include many fell creatures, such as Orcs and Uruk-hai, Trolls and Wargs and other monsters.

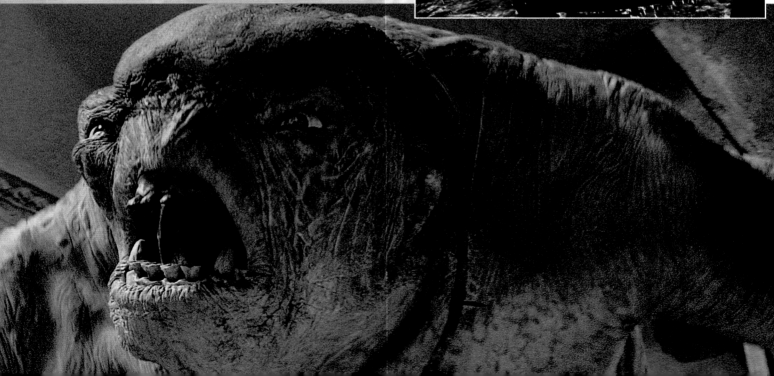

ORCS

"They were once Elves ..."

Orcs are not a natural part of Middle-earth, for they were originally created by the Dark Powers. Long ago, in the First Age, Elves were taken captive, tortured, and mutilated in the dungeons of the Dark Lord, until they had been transformed from the most beautiful and noble of the world's folk into a ruined and terrible new form of life: Orcs. These creatures multiplied until the Dark Lord had grown himself a monstrous army with which to oppress the Free Peoples of the world. Filled with his dark will, they were swarthy and stunted, vicious and evil, and bore little relation to their noble Elven ancestors. Bred in darkness, they hate the light, and when they issue out to do their master's will, it is with demonic energy and cruel blades.

Now, in the Third Age, their kind has spawned such multitudes that they range widely across the world, and are often to be seen as far west as Mirkwood and the edges of the Golden Wood of Lothlórien, a province sacred to the Elves. Others have colonized the great Dwarf-halls of Khazad-dûm.

The foulness of their looks and ferocity of their behavior is matched by the ugliness of their language, which although a degraded form of Westron, the native language of Middle-earth, has in the mouths of the Orcs taken on a vile sound, tainted further by the introduction of words and phrases of the guttural Black Speech of Mordor, whence they originate.

MORIA ORCS

After the Dwarves had abandoned the city of Moria, their ancient home beneath the Misty Mountains, Orcs moved in to occupy the vast halls and passages that were thus left uninhabited. The Orcs of Moria have developed dark skin and pale, protuberant eyes in response to their underground environment, where they scuttle about like insects, using the spikes on their black armor to aid them in their movement up and down the walls and pillars of Khazad-dûm.

URUK-HAI

"Seldom do Orcs journey in the open, under the Sun –
yet these have done so"

Beneath the citadel of Isengard, in the caverns deep beneath its tower, the wizard Saruman has been breeding his own race of super-Orcs — an army to rival that of Sauron, the Dark Lord. By crossing Orcs with Goblin-men, he has created a race of creatures of unparalleled power and brutality. These are the Uruk-hai: taller and straighter than men, massively muscled, black-blooded, and lynx-eyed. Tireless and considerably more intelligent and powerful than the Moria Orcs, they are a fearsome fighting breed, with their viciously efficient straight-bladed weapons and long-range bows. Led by Lurtz, the Uruk-hai of Isengard are easily identifiable by the mark of the White Hand of Saruman that they bear in battle.

THE NAZGÛL

THE NINE SERVANTS OF SAURON

The Nazgûl were once great kings of men to whom Sauron gave nine of the Rings of Power and with them the promise of eternal life and dominion. They took the Rings without question, but their greed blinded them to the Dark Lord's true nature and likely treachery: one by one they fell under the power of the Rings, their bodies and souls corrupted by the Dark Lord's evil until at last they ceased to be human and became instead insubstantial wraiths. Faceless and formless, they have been worn away to terrifying ghouls, shrouded in black robes and armor.

Mounted upon their vast black, flame-eyed steeds, they are known as the Black Riders. Their weapons are not merely swords of steel and flame, nor their maces and morgul-daggers, which carry a deadly poison: their Black Breath also infects with despair and terror all those who are touched by it. No weapons can harm them except for those made by the Elves, and any blade that strikes them will perish.

Recently they have been seen in the vicinity of the Shire.

GOLLUM

"Slyer than a fox and as slippery as a fish"

A lurking presence has dogged the footsteps of the Fellowship since they entered the Mines of Moria, a presence which has been drawn by the evil power of the Ring. This sneaking thing is Gollum; and when Frodo and Sam are separated from their companions amongst the barren, stony slopes of the Emyn Muil they will eventually spy him, spidering around the crags, in search of the Ring.

It is hard to believe, to look at this pale, skinny creature with his long, clinging fingers and toes and his gleaming, bulbous eyes, that once he was a creature not unlike a hobbit. His name then was Sméagol, and he came not from the homey Shire, but was a Stoor, from the lands to the east that border the River Anduin where it runs through the battleground of the Gladden Fields. It was here that Orcs ambushed and overcame Isildur, the King of Men, who carried with him the One Ring that he had cut from the hand of Sauron himself. There the Ring was lost, fallen into the mud at the bottom of the river, and there it lay undisturbed for thousands of years, until the day that Sméagol and his friend Déagol went fishing. Déagol hooked a great fish, which dragged him out of the boat, and when he resurfaced, he had in his hand a golden ring. Sméagol immediately coveted this shiny object; and when Déagol refused to give it to him, Sméagol strangled his friend and stole the Ring away, claiming it as his "birthday present."

"Everywhere we went the Yellowface watched us until we found a hole and we followed it into the mountain, and in the darkness we forgot the sound of trees, the taste of bread, the softness of the wind . . . even our own name"

And thus the Ring began to work its evil influence on the hobbit, making him mutter and gurgle in his throat, so that he became known as "Gollum." It caused him to fear the light and the open air, and drove him out of the sight of the sun into the cave system deep beneath the Misty Mountains, where he lived on raw fish and other things that he caught in its lightless pools. There Gollum stayed, alone except for the Ring, which he called his *Precious*, until Bilbo Baggins chanced upon him. Then the Ring, seeking ever to return to the Dark Lord, insinuated itself into Bilbo's possession, and Bilbo carried it away with him to his home in the Shire. Hating the Ring for leaving him thus, and yet loving it all the while, Gollum was forced to leave his dark retreat and come out into the world to pursue his obsession. However, when he emerged from the caves, Gollum was captured by the Dark Lord's servants and brought to the dungeons beneath the tower of Barad-dûr. There he was tortured as Sauron sought to discover the whereabouts of the Ring, but he managed to escape, and has been hunting his Precious ever since.

"No, no, Master! Don't take the Precious to him! He'll eat us all if he gets it, eat all the world"

And so, once Gollum has been "tamed," caught, and bound by the *hithlain* rope that was given to Sam in Lothlórien, Frodo will find himself making a strange alliance, for he and Gollum share the same goal: to prevent the One Ring from falling into the hands of the Dark Lord. Moreover, Frodo needs a guide through the Land of Shadow, and only Gollum knows the secret ways into Mordor.

THE DEAD MARSHES

"Tricksy lights! Candles of corpses! Wicked lights!"

To the east of the Emyn Muil lies a stretch of marshland that in the last three thousand years has crept its way across the battlefield of Dagorlad. This was the site of the last great conflict against the Dark Lord Sauron, in which the Army of Shadow was defeated and he was brought down, heralding in the Third Age of Middle-earth. Led by Gollum, Frodo and Sam must make their way through these stagnant meres without falling prey to the sinister glamour of the dead who may be glimpsed beneath the murky water. Locked in their armor, weeds threading through their silver hair, there appear to lie beneath the surface of the marshes thousands of dead warriors — Men, Elves, and Orcs — their faces spectral, their bodies bloated and pale. And all around are ghostly lights — will-o'-the-wisps — which, like flickering candles, may tempt the unsuspecting to wander off the safe path, deep into the bog, there to founder and drown.

"You must not look at them when

the candles are lit . . ."

ITHILIEN

In order to avoid direct confrontation with the Dark Lord's army of Orcs, Easterlings, and Mûmakil amassing at the Morannon, the Black Gates of Mordor, Frodo, Sam, and Gollum must approach their destination indirectly. Heading south, they enter Ithilien, the border country between Gondor and Mordor. This area was originally the land of Isildur, son of Elendil, King of Men, but its proximity to Mordor has resulted in the country long being abandoned by its inhabitants. As the travelers make their way through the climbing woods and upland meadows full of rabbit warrens and wildflowers, past waterfalls and swift streams, they will come upon the remnants of that once-great civilization: old roads now unused and overgrown, great statues that have been cast down and crowned with weeds. It is a sad and lovely land, patrolled now only by companies of Rangers who seek to prevent incursions of Orcs and other fell creatures from reaching Gondor.

FARAMIR

Faramir is the second son of Denethor, Steward of Gondor, and the younger brother to Boromir. A stern and commanding man, he is the captain of a band of Rangers who take Frodo and Sam captive as they journey through Ithilien, the border country between Gondor and Mordor. This lovely wooded country is beset by Orcs and other enemies as Sauron's dark forces encroach ever further into the lands of Men. As Captain of the Ithilien Rangers, it falls to Faramir to patrol this dangerous borderland and protect Gondor as best he can from these marauding bands, and from the Dark Lord's spies.

"Since the loss of Boromir he does the duty of two sons …"

Even before taking Frodo and Sam captive and learning the truth of the matter, Faramir has suspected the loss of Boromir, his elder brother. Faramir is a sensitive, discerning man, prone to premonitory dreams, and in one such vision he "saw" the small Elven boat in which Aragorn, Gimli, and Legolas had laid their dead companion, floating on the swell of the great River Anduin, and when he awoke he knew in his heart that his brother was dead. This premonition was then confirmed for him some days later when the silver-banded ox-horn

Boromir carried as the eldest scion of his house was washed up on the riverbank, cloven in two. It was said of this legendary horn that if it were to be blown anywhere within the ancient boundaries of the realm of Gondor, its call would not go unheeded. But when Boromir fell to Uruk-hai arrows while defending Merry and Pippin, he was beyond the bounds of the ancient kingdom, and the faint echo of the horn was dim and distant.

Their father is Lord Denethor, the Steward of Gondor, one of a long line who has held the kingdom in readiness for the return of Isildur's heir. Denethor waits in despair for news of his eldest son, despising his younger son all the while, which is a bitter burden for Faramir to bear.

Faramir, like his brother, is tempted to take the Ring to use on behalf of his people. It is among the embattled ruins of the ancient city of Osgiliath that Faramir must decide the fate of the Ring, and its bearer, Frodo Baggins. In his hands lies the future of the Free Peoples of Middle-earth.

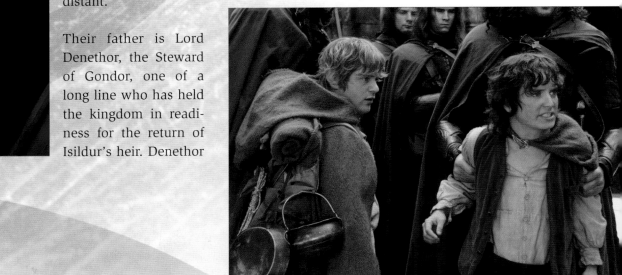

MERRY, PIPPIN, AND THE URUK-HAI

"Kill all, but not the Halflings...They have some Elvish weapon.

The Master wants it for the war ..."

When the Uruk-hai warriors fell upon the Fellowship on the slopes below Amon Hen, Meriadoc Brandybuck and his cousin, Peregrin Took, defended themselves valiantly, even though it was the first time they had borne arms in battle. Aragorn and Gimli fought the Orcish attackers in fierce hand-to-hand combat with sword and axe, and Legolas proved deadly with his Elven longbow; but despite the bravery of the companions the Uruk-hai proved too many and too strong, and the Fellowship was sundered. The fearsome

Uruk leader, Lurtz, loosed a rain of arrows that killed Boromir, son of Denethor, and then the ambushers captured Merry and Pippin, recognizing them as belonging to the race of halflings known as hobbits. They had been charged by their master, Saruman the White, with the task of finding a certain hobbit bearing a rare and powerful artifact, and bringing both safely to Isengard: but knowing neither the identity of the hobbit in question, nor the nature of the thing the wizard covets, they mistakenly believe Merry or Pippin is the hobbit they seek.

"We are the fighting Uruk-hai … the servants of Saruman the Wise, the White Hand …"

Saruman's Uruk-hai have been bred for power, speed, and brutality. Great swart, massive-muscled, slant-eyed beasts, they were birthed in the caves beneath the fortress at Isengard, tormented in order to forge their cruel spirits, and fed upon unspeakable things. They bear upon them Saruman's mark — a white hand painted on their shields and faces. Tireless and determined, they can run through the day as well as the night, unlike other Orcs, which dislike feeling the sun's eye upon them and prefer to move in darkness. Their leader — now that the master's greatest creation, Lurtz, lies dead at Aragorn's hand — is Uglúk. Because of their small size, the hobbits are easy to carry so the Uruk-hai make swift progress toward their goal.

FANGORN FOREST

"This forest is old, very old, and full of memory …"

At the southern end of the Misty Mountains there lies a wild and ancient woodland, the remnant of the vast woods that once covered all of this part of the land in the Elder Days. Inside, it may appear dark and forbidding to strangers, full of shadows and strange shapes. Trees stand, rank upon rank, in every direction; some tall and slender and straight, their lithe limbs reaching for the light, while others are gnarled and bent by age, their bark all ridged and scored. Many are clothed in lichen, as if with great beards and whiskers; others are covered in dry brown leaves, and have long-fingered twigs, like hands that may clutch. And sometimes, out of the corner of the eye, it may appear that they have moved not as trees move, with the passing of the wind but of their own accord. It is an eerie place to travelers who do not know it well, and can be dangerous to those who are not kind to trees. It is not wise to cut live wood to make a campfire in Fangorn Forest.

"Saruman used to walk in these woods,

but now he has a mind of metal and wheels"

In the south, smoke rises from the factories of Isengard. There, the great Forest has been cut down in swathes: hewn tree stumps mark its ravaged slopes. The wizard Saruman, Chief of the Order of the Istari, who came to Middle-earth to aid the Free Peoples, has been corrupted by his quest for knowledge and power, so that now he thinks to challenge the Dark Lord himself. Driven at first by Sauron's command and lately by his own ambition, he has been systematically destroying the woods that border his fortress at Isengard in order to provide fuel and timber for his many projects of war — fuel for the fires in which dark armor and blades are forged for his great army; timber for siege towers and ladders and battering rams. The trees of Fangorn and their protectors and herds, the mysterious Ents, will not be forgiving of such wanton destruction.

ENTS

"Ere iron was found or tree was hewn,

When young was mountain under moon;

Ere ring was made, or wrought was woe,

It walked the forests long ago."

Inside Fangorn Forest, Merry and Pippin — having escaped their captors — will meet one of Middle-earth's most ancient and extraordinary inhabitants. Because he is as tall as a tree, as gnarled as a tree, as covered in moss and leaves and lichens as any tree, it is easy to mistake him for a tree. But Treebeard, or Fangorn (for he shares his name with the forest in which he walks) is a member of the Onodrim, or Ents — guardians and tree-herds to the great forests of Middle-earth.

"The oldest living thing that still walks beneath the Sun upon this Middle-earth"

Treebeard is the oldest and wisest of the Ents: for three Ages he has walked Middle-earth, tending the trees and watching the peoples of the world come and go, teaching them the ways of plant and tree and flower.

The name "Ent" was given to the Onodrim by the people of Rohan, in whose language it means "giant"; and gigantic they are, standing at fourteen feet and more. They are clad in a substance much like bark, being gray and brown and green and ridged and wrinkled by age. Their fingers are like twigs and their great feet have seven long, gnarled toes that resemble nothing so much as tree-roots. Ents are very slow-moving, and slow-thinking. An Entmoot, or council, can last for days at a time, for Ents like to consider matters carefully; but if at last they are roused to anger, their fury is formidable, and when it is combined with their ancient strength, neither fortress nor army can withstand them. And the Ents of Fangorn will not look kindly upon the ravages of Saruman the White, who has ripped their kin from the land surrounding Isengard root by root, or cut them down where they have for centuries stood in peace.

THE MASTER OF ISENGARD

"The White Wizard is cunning..."

Saruman the White, foremost of the Istari wizards who came to Middle-earth to guide all the Free Peoples against the growing evil of Sauron, Lord of Mordor, has himself developed a great appetite for power in this world. For long years he has studied the ways of the Dark Lord, seeking out arcane knowledge from ancient texts, acquiring magical lore and craft, readying himself to make his move. His stronghold at Isengard, long ago acquired by the wizard as part of his grand scheme, stands in a crucial strategic location: guarding the Gap of Rohan between the White Mountains and the Misty Mountains; and what was once a fortress built to ensure the safety of the Kingdom of Rohan has now

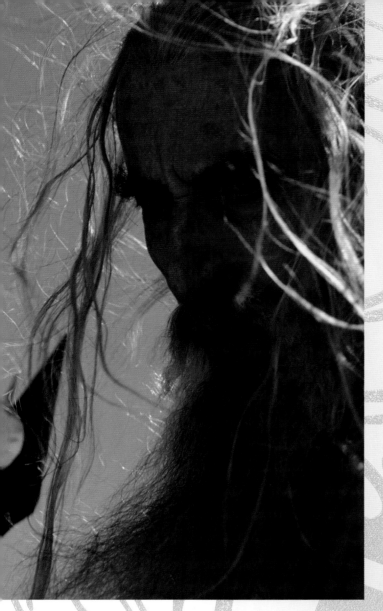

become a base from which enemies will issue out to engulf it. For in the caverns beneath his stronghold Saruman has created an army of Uruk-hai — Orcs bred with Goblin-Men to make them powerful, cruel, and tireless. He has marked them with his own device, that of the White Hand, and these creatures roam freely throughout the lands surrounding Isengard, killing at will.

"…his spies are everywhere"

Having learned from Gandalf the Grey the whereabouts of the One Ring, Saruman is determined to acquire it and use it for his own purposes. He sent an elite band of his Uruk-hai warriors to capture Frodo Baggins, the hobbit Ringbearer; but when the Uruks set upon the Fellowship beneath Amon Hen, Frodo escaped them and it was Merry and Pippin who were taken captive.

Foiled in this venture, he will launch his monstrous army of Uruk-hai, Wild Men, Orcs, and Wargs upon the Kingdom of Rohan, the country he has weakened from within by the use of his spy and weapon, Gríma Wormtongue, who has poisoned the mind of King Théoden, rendering him incapable of action and decision.

THE PALANTÍR

The palantíri are the eight legendary seeing-stones, crystal globes made by the Elves, which could enable a person of strong will to view scenes far away in time and space, especially in the proximity of another seeing-stone. Most have been lost down the ages, but one of the surviving stones fell into the clutches of the Dark Lord Sauron, which made all the other palantíri dangerous to use. Another was housed in Orthanc, where Saruman found it and strove for mastery of it, but this has made him susceptible to the will of Sauron.

THE SHADOW OF SARUMAN

Saruman has established great factories and foundries at Isengard — furnaces and smithies and armories to forge weapons and armor and engines of war — turning what was once a beautiful landscape of wooded valleys, groves, and tumbling streams into a barren wasteland of brambles, sere grass, and thorns. Rotting stumps mark the death of trees that have been felled and carried away to fuel his evil fires. Pungent, colored smoke billows into the skies around Orthanc, poisoning the very air. Saruman's depredations can be seen for miles, a constant reminder to the Ents of the murder done to their wards, the trees, and a warning to the Horse-lords of Rohan of the danger that lurks on their doorstep.

THE PURSUIT

After the conflict below Amon Hen during which the Fellowship of the Ring was sundered, Aragorn made the hard decision that instead of accompanying the Ringbearer and Samwise Gamgee, he, Legolas, and Gimli should attempt to catch up with and rescue the missing hobbits, Merry and Pippin, from the marauding band of Uruk-hai that carried them off.

"Some evil gives speed to these creatures

and sets its will against us"

The Uruk-hai that are heading back toward Isengard and their master, the wizard Saruman the White, have been bred for power and speed, and unlike other Orcs have little fear of the light of the sun: the pursuers must somehow track them and run hard for several days and nights across rough terrain if they are to save their friends.

"Where sight fails the earth may bring us rumor.

The land must groan under their hated feet"

Three days and nights' pursuit brings Aragorn, Legolas, and Gimli to the Plains of Rohan, where they discover a heap of smoldering Orc and Uruk-hai bodies on the edge of Fangorn Forest, evidence of a slaughter by deadly assailants. But there is no sign of the missing hobbits. Within the Forest, however, there will be a remarkable and unlooked-for reunion.

GANDALF THE WHITE

"I come back to you now, at the turn of the tide"

As the Fellowship, pursued by hordes of Orcs, fled through the Mines of Moria — the ancient kingdom of the Dwarves — a great, distant rumbling was heard; then the ground began to shake and a fierce and fiery light came snaking through the labyrinth of tunnels. The air became hot. A creature of the ancient world had been roused: a fire-demon, a Balrog known as Durin's Bane. Terrified by its presence, the Orcs scattered in their hundreds, swarming up the vast pillars and out across the halls of Khazad-dûm. Shrouded by fire it came, black smoke wreathing about its dark body and horned head. Armed with a flaming sword and a many-thonged whip, it raced toward them.

Gandalf the Grey ordered the rest of the Fellowship to save themselves by crossing the narrow bridge across the abyss while he waited in the middle of the span to hold the demon at bay. The Fellowship, looking back from the safety of the Dimrill side of the bridge, saw how the Balrog towered above the wizard. They saw the demon's fire answered by the white fire of Gandalf's sword, Glamdring. They saw the wizard strike the bridge with his staff; they saw the span break. They saw how the Balrog, falling, wrapped its whip around the wizard's legs and dragged him down with it into the abyss. And then they saw no more and believed him lost.

But Gandalf did not perish. Down he fell with the Balrog, far below the living earth to the utmost foundations of stone, fighting all the way. When freezing waters engulfed them the Balrog's fire was quenched, and then Gandalf pursued it through the darkest of tunnels. The demon fled from the wizard, up the secret ways of Khazad-dûm until it reached the Endless Stair that brought the two

combatants all the way up to Durin's Tower, carved into the rock of Zirak-zigil. There, where the stair came out at a dizzying height above the mists of the world, the Balrog's fire sprang back to life, and there Gandalf fought him long and hard, so that it appeared that fire and lightning struck the mountain, until at last the fire-demon fell from that high place and found its death.

On that cold mountain, as the stars wheeled overhead, darkness claimed Gandalf. There he lay, lost and stranded, straying out of thought and time. But he did not die, for his task on Middle-earth was not yet done and he was sent back. When Aragorn, Legolas, and Gimli search for the lost hobbits in Fangorn Forest, they come upon an old man whom they mistake at first for Saruman, for, under his ragged cloak he is dressed all in white. White, too, are his hair and his beard and his staff. A bright light is in his eye.

Gandalf the Grey is no more; now he has returned, full of power, as Gandalf the White.

THE KINGDOM
OF ROHAN

To the north of Gondor lies the realm of Rohan, known by its people as the Riddermark. It is bordered to the west by the Gap and Fords of Isen (beyond which lies the wizard Saruman's stronghold of Isengard), by the River Limlight in the north, by the Entwash that flows out of Fangorn Forest in the east; and by the White Mountains in the south. The wide, grassy plains of the Riddermark stretch for league upon league in all directions like a great green ocean, and it is here that for generations the people of Rohan — the Rohirrim — have bred the magnificent horses for which they are famed throughout Middle-earth, earning them the title of "the Horse-lords."

THE ROHIRRIM

"Where now the horse and the rider? Where is the horn that was blowing?

Where is the helm and the hauberk, and the bright hair flowing?

Where is the hand on the harpstring, and the red fire glowing?

Where is the spring and the harvest and the tall corn growing?

They have passed like rain on the mountain, like a wind in the meadow;

The days have gone down in the West behind the hills into shadow."

The Horse-lords of Rohan are a proud and ancient people of the race of Men. Stern-faced and handsome they are, brave and generous of spirit. They write no books, but they make many songs celebrating their deeds in battle, or the fine horses they breed. The Riders of Rohan, mounted on their fine Riddermark horses, wear burnished skirts of mail to their knees, and carry tall spears of ash and painted shields slung at their backs. They wear their flaxen hair long and in braids, under their decorated helms. Tall and fierce, they are well-versed in the arts of war, as needs must, for ever since winning their lands they have had to defend them on every border — from raids by Orcs and Uruk-hai (who have lately encroached as far as the Fords of Isen, there mortally wounding King Théoden's heir, Théodred); from the sea-pirates of Umbar in the south; from the Wild Men and Dunlendings whom they long ago drove into the hill country; and, most disturbingly, from Mordor.

And while they are not yet openly at war with Mordor, they feel the chill of its shadow creeping ever westwards, which makes them wary of all strangers: so when Aragorn, Legolas, and Gimli traverse their lands in search of their missing companions, they may not meet with the welcome they expect.

KING THÉODEN

"Théoden no longer recognizes friend from foe . . . not even his own kin"

Once a great warrior-king of the proud Rohirrim, the Horse-lords of Rohan, and much beloved by his people, now Théoden sits slumped on his throne in the feast-hall of Meduseld, a man broken in spirit, weighed down by what appears to be premature age and feebleness. In his youth he was tall and proud, strong and stern, as is the nature of the Men of the Riddermark, but tragedy visited his house, striking first his wife, Elfhild, who was lost in childbirth, bearing him his only son, Théodred; then his sister's husband fell to Orcs and his wife, Théoden's beloved younger sister Théodwyn, sickened and died of grief, leaving behind two orphans, Éomer and Éowyn. These two children Théoden should have cared for as a father, but he was bowed down by his losses.

Then the wizard Saruman, whose lands border those of Rohan, saw his opportunity and engaged the services of a sneaking spy — Gríma, son of Gálmód — known as "Wormtongue." For years Gríma has wormed his way into the King's mind, filling it with evil counsel, preparing the way for Saruman to take over the land of Rohan. The wizard's army of Uruk-hai and Orcs encroach ever further into the Riddermark; yet all the while Théoden has sunk further into despair and torpor, unable to take action against these incursions, or even to recognize the dangers. When his sister-son, Éomer, warned his king against Gríma, he became angry with the lad and banished him, to Wormtongue's great satisfaction.

War is advancing upon the peoples of the Riddermark. Mordor's influence creeps ever closer, and Wild Men and Dunlendings, Orcs and Uruk-hai are invading from the west, killing all in their path. Rohan needs its king now more than ever in its history; Théoden of the Rohirrim must be raised from his stupor and once more take up arms and lead his people in battle against the forces of evil, or all will be lost.

THE COMPANIONS' JOURNEY

EDORAS

"Golden, too, are the posts of its doors"

The chief settlement of the Riddermark is Edoras, the Courts of Rohan, situated on top of a rocky outcrop in the lee of the White Mountains, its circumference protected by a mighty wall and wooden palisade. King Théoden, Lord of Rohan, resides there in Meduseld, the Golden Hall, the high-house of the kingdom, a sumptuous feasting hall thatched as if with gold, its pillars and beams all carved in the complex and beautiful style of the Rohirrim, incorporating a myriad of twining, gripping beasts and horse motifs to mark the great love and respect the Horse-lords have for their noble animals.

GRÍMA WORMTONGUE

"You were once a man of Rohan ..."

Gríma, son of Gálmód, close counselor to King Théoden of Rohan, is a pale, stooped, cringing man who dresses always in black robes. He is known by all but the King as "Wormtongue" — for all but the Lord of Rohan see him for what he is — a poisonous viper in the nest of Edoras. Day by day he has poured treacherous words into Théoden's ear, sapping his will and the clear sight by which a king must govern; isolating him from all good influences. The death of Théodred, the King's son, brought home to be tended for the wounds he sustained at the Fords of Isen, may also lie at Gríma's hand. He has even taken Herugrim, the King's sword and the symbol of his power, into his own keeping, and has turned Théoden against all those who might urge the King to war — in particular his nephew, Éomer, Third Marshal of the Mark.

For Gríma is the spy of the wizard Saruman the White, master of neighboring Isengard, planted in the court of the King in order to weaken him and bring him down. Saruman wishes to subvert the rule of Rohan, and he has promised his spy a special prize when at last the realm of the Horse-lords lies within his power: possession of the beautiful Lady Éowyn.

"Too long have you watched her under your eyelids and haunted her steps"

ÉOMER

"We welcomed guests kindly in the better days,
but in these times the unbidden stranger finds us swift and hard"

As Aragorn, Legolas, and Gimli pursue the band of Uruk-hai who captured and bore away their hobbit companions, Merry and Pippin, they enter the lands of the Riddermark. There, they come upon a group of fierce horsemen, the Riders of Rohan. Their captain is a tall, stern man, steel-helmed, mail-shirted, and well-armed. His name is Éomer, son of Éomund, and he is the Third Marshal of the Riddermark, nephew to Théoden, King of Rohan. With his men, and against the orders of his lord — who has fallen prey to the evil counsels of Gríma Wormtongue — he is out hunting Orcs, and any others who may be enemies to the kingdom.

"I serve only the Lord of the Mark, Théoden King, son of Thengel"

Gríma, the spy, has been poisoning the mind of the King against those who would serve him honestly, and as a result he has persuaded Théoden to regard his brave and faithful nephew as a dangerous traitor who would stir up conflict for his own advancement.

"Put your trust in Éomer,
rather than a man of crooked mind"

But the scales could fall from the Lord of the Mark's eyes, if he is released from the treacherous bewitchment that has bound him for so long. With enemies closing in from all sides, King Théoden must realize that Éomer — a fine soldier, valiant warrior, and a man of wisdom and understanding — is exactly the kind of hero the Kingdom of Rohan seeks in its hour of need.

ÉOWYN

"You are the daughter of kings, a shield maiden of Rohan …"

Éowyn, Lady of Rohan, is the daughter of Éomund, Marshal of the Mark, who was lost to Orc-attack when she was only a girl, and King Théoden's sister, Théodwyn, who succumbed to grief at the loss of her husband. King Théoden brought Éowyn and her elder brother Éomer to Edoras, and there raised them as his own, until he fell beneath the sinister influence of Gríma Wormtongue and became old, infirm, and befuddled before his time.

"Fair and cold, like a morning of pale spring …"

The people of Rohan are by nature fierce and grave, but Éowyn's upbringing has weighed heavily upon her: there has been little carefree pleasure in her life, and laughter does not come easily to her. Willowy and fair, with her pale skin and her long hair like a river of gold, she is undeniably beautiful,

but she has a chilly aspect and a regard as stern as steel. Nevertheless, Gríma Wormtongue is captivated by Éowyn; and his master, the wizard Saruman, has promised her to him when the realm of Rohan falls beneath his power. But when Éowyn sets her eyes upon the Lord Aragorn, heir of kings, her heart is lost; albeit his is given to Arwen Evenstar, Lady of Rivendell.

The Lady of Rohan wears an ancient sword, and she has as much skill in its use as any man. Soon she will have the need to use it.

HORSES OF THE RIDDERMARK

The horses that have for generations been bred by the Men of Rohan are big and strong and clean-limbed, with coats that glisten and long, flowing manes and tails. Swift and powerful, they can run like the wind. Great herds of them roamed the eastern part of the Riddermark, watched over by nomadic herdsmen, but lately because of the growing threat from Mordor, they have been withdrawn into the interior for safety.

SHADOWFAX

Chief of the Mearas, the greatest horses of Rohan and "lord of all horses," Shadowfax knows the speech of Men and has the power to outrun even the horses of the Nazgûl. He is so named because his coat is silver-gray.

BREGO

"Stille nu, faeste ... Hwaet nemnath the?"

Quiet now, steady ... What do they call you?

A fine bay stallion survived the skirmish at the Fords of Isen where his rider, the Lord Théodred, was wounded, and returned to the stables at Edoras. Since then he has been wild and will suffer no one to approach him until Aragorn, son of Arathorn, comes to him and quiets him in his own language of Rohirric and that of the Elves, for Aragorn was raised for a time in Rivendell. The horse is called Brego, in honor of the second King of Rohan, and a strong bond will be forged between the horse and his new rider; a bond that will serve Aragorn well when Orcs attack the company on the road to Dunharrow.

THE HARROWING OF ROHAN

"He has taken Orcs into his service, and Wolf-riders, and evil Men, and he has closed the Gap against us, so that we are likely to be beset both east and west"

Once the grasslands of Rohan rolled across the plains like a great, green sea, and the Horse-lords kept their herds and studs in the east of the realm, their herdsmen living a peaceful, nomadic existence, moving from grazing ground to grazing ground and from village to village; but since Mordor's shadow has lengthened into that quarter the land there now lies empty, brooding under an ominous silence, a silence that does not seem to be the quiet of peace.

From the west comes another threat, from beyond the Gap of Rohan, the pass that lies between the White Mountains and the Misty Mountains and acts as a gateway into the kingdom. The Gap is guarded by the fortress at Isengard, dwelling-place of Saruman the White, who has for long professed himself a friend to the Rohirrim and their king. But Orcs and Uruk-hai have increasingly been making forays into Rohan through the Gap. And not just Orcs: for his own purposes, it seems, Saruman has exhorted the ancient enemies of Rohan — the Wild Men and the Dunlendings, who long ago were driven off their land and into the hills — to rise up and join with his own vile army.

"They do not come to destroy Rohan's crops or villages — they come to destroy its people ... down to the last child"

The land of Rohan is being harrowed: settlements are ravaged, the buildings put to the torch; men, women, and children cut down as they flee. Rohirrim warriors try to hold back these evil forces and defend their people, but they are cruelly outnumbered. Théodred, son of Théoden, was injured in battle at the Fords of Isen, and many of his men lost their lives; now the survivors of such conflicts and thousands of refugees from burned villages must flee toward Dunharrow, and seek safe haven in the impregnable stronghold of Helm's Deep.

WARG-RIDERS

During the Third Age of Middle-earth, the Wargs of Rhovanion made an alliance with the Orcs of the Misty Mountains. When Saruman the White began to draw together his army from the many enemies of the Free Peoples of Middle-earth, the Wargs and their Orc allies came down from the mountains the further to strengthen the wizard's forces.

Because of the great size of the wolf-like Wargs — at least as big as the horses of Rohan — the Orcs used them to ride them into battle. The Wargs are extremely vicious and efficient hunters, able to cover vast distances tirelessly in their search for prey. Because of this, they represent a huge threat to any who would cross the plains of Rohan undefended.

ARWEN'S CHOICE

"I looked into your future, and I saw death"

Thousands of years before the events that are now unfolding, an Elven maiden and a mortal man came together, fell in love, and pledged their troth, in desperate times, in defiance of their different races, and against all the odds. Their names were Beren and Lúthien.

Beren was a hero among men, a scion of the house of Barahir. One day, in the forest of Neldoreth he saw a figure dancing, and so beautiful was she that he was struck dumb. She was Lúthien, daughter of Thingol of the eternal race of Elves; and from that moment Beren lost his heart; although he knew that if she were to forsake her people to be with him, she must also forsake her immortality.

In the Third Age of Middle-earth, another mortal man chanced on an Elven maiden in the woods at Rivendell, and she was in her own time of all living things the most fair; for she was Arwen, the descendant of Lúthien. Like Beren, the man who spied her there was doomed to love from the first moment he saw her; this was Aragorn, son of Arathorn, and he was descended from Beren's line, as

token of which he wore the Ring of Barahir. Aragorn did not know that this maid was the daughter of Elrond who had raised him in Rivendell since he was a child, for during all the years in which Aragorn had been in Rivendell, Arwen had been in Lothlórien with the Lady Galadriel, her mother's mother.

Although he perceived the love that lay between Aragorn and Arwen, the Lord Elrond would not permit their betrothal: for his daughter was fated to leave the world of men and pass with him into the Undying Lands, there to live forever as an immortal; while Aragorn's shoulders were to bear another destiny entirely: to fight the forces of evil in the War of the Ring and to live out his short span as a mortal man in Middle-earth.

HELM'S DEEP

Helm's Deep, named for Helm Hammerhand, the hero of ancient wars who made his refuge there, lies in a gorge that winds its way below three-peaked Thrihyrne in the northern White Mountains. It has long been the defensive center of the Westfold and the kings of Rohan have over the ages constructed a vast and seemingly impregnable system of fortification in the gorge, including defensive walls and keeps.

"No army has ever breached the Deeping Wall nor set foot inside the Hornburg.

Not while Men of Rohan defend it ..."

The entrance to the Deep is commanded by Helm's Gate, a tall wooden gate now rotting with age and, upon a great spur of rock, the towering structure of the Hornburg, a massive-walled keep said to have been built by the hands of giants in the days of the sea-kings of Gondor. From the keep to the mouth of Helm's Gate runs the Deeping Wall, a great fortified wall, wide enough to enable four men at once to stand abreast the top, shielded by its tall parapet and reached by stairs running down from the outer court of the Hornburg. Three flights of steps lead up to the wall from the Deep behind, but the outer surface is smooth and unscalable. Beneath the Wall lies Helm's Dike, a vast defensive earthwork a mile or more long, cut through only by a stream that runs through a deep culvert.

"Saruman's arm will have grown long indeed if he thinks he can reach us here"

Beneath Helm's Deep lie the Glittering Caves of Aglarond, a spectacular cavern system that is truly one of Middle-earth's natural wonders, and has proved in times past to be a safe haven when the Kingdom of Rohan is under attack.

PREPARING FOR BATTLE

Massively outnumbered by a horde of ten thousand Uruk-hai marching on the gorge from Isengard, the remaining members of the Fellowship and their comrades must prepare for the onslaught of the enemy by donning armor and making ready their weapons. Even though Helm's Deep has proved impregnable in past conflicts, its gates are now rotting and its defenders are few. The odds against the people of Rohan and its allies are appalling: no matter how valiantly they fight, they can surely never triumph.

"I am of the world of Men and these are my people: I will die as one of them ..."

Over his tunic, Aragorn puts on a short-sleeved shirt of heavy chainmail and protects his forearms with the tooled leather vambraces once worn by Boromir of Gondor. His sword is keen-edged. Legolas, prince of the Mirkwood Elves, dons armor for the first time in his life. He carries two lethal white knives at his belt, his great Galadhrim long-bow, and the peacock-decorated quiver of arrows

given to him by the Lady Galadriel in Lothlórien. The Dwarf-warrior, Gimli, son of Glóin, remains battle-dressed in his own leather armor and impressive iron helmet, and carries five fearsome battle-axes.

> *"Arise now, arise, Riders of Théoden!*
>
> *Dire deeds awake, dark is it eastward.*
>
> *Let horse be bridled, horn be sounded!*
>
> *Forth, Eorlingas!"*

King Théoden of Rohan is arrayed in full Rohirrim wargear, including a mighty helmet, engraved breastplate, and mailshirt. He carries his greatsword Herugrim. Beside him, the Royal Guard of Rohan, led by Gamling, are similarly arrayed.

Just a few hundred refugees from the settlements that have been harrowed by Orcs and Wild Men throughout Rohan have made it through to Helm's Deep. These few will be fitted out for battle in the Hornburg armory. They are a motley bunch of old men and untested boys; but all are ready to fight to the death to defend their kingdom, even though they are vastly outnumbered and their defense appears doomed.

Down in the Glittering Caves the women and the children take refuge, where they will be defended by Éowyn, shield-maiden of Rohan.

The sky is darkening: a storm is brewing...

ELVES AND MEN

"The world is changing. I feel it in the water. I feel it in the earth and I smell it in the air. Our time here is over …"

The Elves last fought alongside Men to combat the forces of evil at the Battle of Dagorlad, which brought about the downfall of Sauron and ended the Second Age. Now, in the Third Age, Sauron has steadily rebuilt his strength and his armies, while the Elves have dwindled, both in number and in their influence upon the peoples of Middle-earth. In increasing numbers, they have made the decision to pass out of this war-torn, sorrowful world over the Sea and into the Undying Lands, where they may enjoy their immortality in peace and bliss.

"In days of old our people stood beside the King of Gondor …"

For many of the Elven race, the affairs of Men have become a distant concern, a matter of history, almost of legend. Since Isildur struck the Ring from the Dark Lord's hand at Dagorlad and was himself corrupted by its power, three thousand years have passed, and the bloodline of Gondor has fallen into decay. Little is known of the ability of Isildur's heir, Aragorn, to unite the peoples of Middle-earth, and few Elves any longer trust to the strength of Men. Likewise, the fate of Frodo and his quest to destroy the Ring does not touch them deeply: even with the finest of intentions, such trials of courage are likely to come to nothing.

But unless Sauron's Eye is distracted by the imminent battle at Helm's Deep, his full attention will at once be turned upon the discovery and capture of the Ringbearer, and if the Dark Lord regains possession of the One Ring, his might will be overwhelming and his shadow will fall across all of Middle-earth. Yet there are so few defenders to withstand the vast Orcish army being unleashed upon Helm's Deep that — without the intervention and alliance of the Elves — the heroic distraction will surely be fatally brief.

Elrond, Lord of Rivendell, the Lady Galadriel, and Lord Celeborn of the Golden Wood, and their captain, Haldir of the Galadhrim, must debate long and hard as to the best course of action to pursue. Upon their decision may rest the success or failure of the entire enterprise.

"We have seen too many defeats, too many fruitless victories, to trust again to the strength of Men"

THE ENEMY

"Za dashu snaku Zigur, Durgbu nazgshu, Durgbu dashshu!

Hail, Sauron, Lord of the Rings, Lord of the Earth!"

Ranged against the defenders of Helm's Deep is a warhost ten thousand strong made up of Orcs, on foot and mounted upon Wargs — great beasts resembling giant wolves — and renegade Wild Men from the hill country of Dunland. But, most significantly of all, there are the fearsome Uruk-hai, Orcs that have been bred with Goblin-Men by the wizard Saruman in the caverns below Isengard. And amongst these there are legions of crossbow archers, longbow archers, and berserkers — monstrous warriors apparently immune to pain and fear who will lead the assault on Helm's Deep.

"It is an army bred for one purpose: to destroy the world of Men."

THE KINGDOM OF GONDOR

South and east of the Kingdom of Rohan, and closest of all to Mordor, lies Gondor, the great kingdom of Men which was founded by Elendil in the Second Age of Middle-earth. In elder days, it counted amongst its chief cities Osgiliath, Minas Tirith, and Minas Ithil and the ports of Dol Amroth and Pelargir; but Minas Ithil was lost to the Nazgûl and is now known as Minas Morgul, and Osgiliath has become little more than an outpost of war. Through millennia, war and plague have decreased Gondor's power and its population, and after the failing of Elendil's line, the kingdom has had no king. Gondor is no longer the mighty and glorious realm it once was.

MINAS TIRITH

"Mordor: this city has dwelt ever in sight of that shadow"

Where the White Mountains come to an end in the great peak of Mount Mindolluin, there lies Minas Tirith, the City of Kings. It is a vast and elegant city, built in seven levels of white stone that have been carved into the hill so that it looks less a creation of men's hands, but a settlement hewn out of the very bones of the earth by giants. Each level is ringed by a wall and battlement and a gate set into each wall at different points, so that the paved road that climbs toward the seventh level zigzags its way to the summit. The topmost circle rises more than seven hundred feet above the Great Gate that is set into the first circle, and the view downward is sheer and vertiginous.

At the summit lies the Citadel, which contains the High Court, the Place of the Fountain, and the White Tower of Ecthelion, where the white banner of the Stewards flutters a thousand feet above the plain.

Minas Tirith is a mighty fortification: apparently impregnable, for there is no access into the city save by the Great Gate of Gondor at its base, which is well guarded indeed. At its back Mount Mindolluin rises sheer and its lower skirts are hedged with ramparts right up to the unscalable precipice. Its walls are high and massively thick, unconquerable by steel or fire, and its battlements afford cover to archers: it is the greatest stronghold in all of Middle-earth.

"It is before the walls of Minas Tirith that the doom of our time will be decided!"

THE GUARDS OF THE CITADEL

Tall ships and tall kings

Three times three

What brought they from the foundered land

Over the flowing sea?

Seven stars and seven stones

And one white tree.

The Guards of the Citadel are robed in black, and their glittering silver helmets are tall and high-crowned and are made from mithril, that most beautiful and priceless of metals, mined by the Dwarves. Light and hard, it could be beaten like copper and polished like glass, and its sheen would never tarnish. These marvelous helmets have long cheek-guards that fit close to the face, and above the cheek-guards are set the white wings of sea-birds, in memory of the days of yore, when Elendil and the ancestors of men sailed to Middle-earth from Númenor, the westernmost of all mortal lands. The guards' black surcoats are embroidered in white with a blossoming tree beneath a silver crown and seven stars. This is the livery of all the heirs of Elendil and is now worn in all of Middle-earth only by the Citadel Guards of Minas Tirith. The seven stars represent the stars figured on the sails of the ships, bearing the seven seeing-stones, which brought Elendil and his people from Númenor.

THE WHITE TREE

Isildur, son of Elendil, who saw his father die on the field of battle against Sauron, and who cut from the Dark Lord's hand the One Ring, planted a sapling from the seeds brought from his homeland in Númenor in memory of his brother, Anárion. But in later days, the tree withered and died, so that now before the pretty fountain in the white-paved court-yard it is a sorrowful sight indeed; black and broken and barren, a fitting symbol indeed for the kingless realm of Gondor in its sad decline.

THE STEWARDS OF THE KINGS

When the line of the Kings failed, the Stewards became the official rulers in Gondor and passed the title down from father to son for hundreds of years. Although appointed to hold the kingdom in charge until the rightful king shall come and claim the throne, such a great span of time has now elapsed that there is no longer any belief that a king shall return, and the Stewards have become increasingly arrogant and king in all but name.

Nevertheless, the Stewards never sit on the ancient throne of Gondor itself, but on a plain, black stone chair at its foot in the chilly, high-vaulted great hall of Minas Tirith. They wear no crown or robes of office and carry only a simple white stave as a token of their rule, rather than any kind of scepter; and their banner — which flies from the top of the Tower of Ecthelion — is of plain white, whereas the royal banner, like the insignia of the Citadel Guards, has a sable ground and bears the image of a white tree capped by seven stars.

"The rule of Gondor is mine, and no other's!"

The current Steward of Gondor is Denethor, son of Ecthelion, father to Boromir and Faramir. He is an old man now, and time and grief have etched deep lines on his proud face. Denethor has learned too much of the lore of the world — from the great library of Minas Tirith, and from gazing into the surviving seeing-stone in the White Tower. As a result, he knows more than any save Gandalf of the horrors they face in the War for Middle-earth, but the peril of possessing such knowledge is that it can give way to despair, and thence to madness.

"Boromir was loyal to me and no wizard's pupil!"

The discovery of the death of his eldest son, Boromir, has already diverted his noble mind from a sane course, and in his grief he has turned against his younger son, Faramir, so that it seems there is nothing the young Captain of Gondor can do to win his father's approval. That

the fallen city of Osgiliath against overwhelming odds is surely a fool's mission and one that must surely result in Faramir's death.

THE TOMBS OF THE STEWARDS

"The houses of the dead are no places for the living"

On the Hallows, the silent shoulder of rock between the mountain and the citadel, there is a great domed chamber in which no breath stirs. Inside, draped with shadow, rows of tables carved from marble line this grim hall, and on each sarcophagus lies a sleeping form, hands folded on its chest. These are the Tombs of the Stewards, where the remains of the dead lie interred in crumbling grandeur like gray ghosts. It is a place of great veneration, for the people of Gondor now seem to accord more reverence to the dead than to the living.

Faramir allowed Frodo Baggins to carry the One Ring into Mordor, rather than bringing it back to Gondor to be used as a weapon in the war against Sauron, is something his father cannot forgive. Yet to send his younger son out to retake

OSGILIATH

"No army of Sauron has ever crossed the Anduin,

not while men of Gondor have held the passage of the river"

On either bank of the Anduin stand the ruins of a once-mighty city, the two sides of which are linked by an ancient stone bridge that spans the Great River. Known by the Gondorian people as Osgiliath, it was called "the Citadel of the Stars" by the Elves, and in the elder days was the capital city of the kingdom of Gondor.

Over the passing of the centuries, after the depredations of war and plague had taken their toll on the population, the folk of Gondor gradually moved away from Osgiliath, abandoning it to the forces of age and time until little of its magnificence and grace remained. Towers were cast down, statues tumbled, weeds sprang up through the cobbled stones of its streets. Now, as a new and terrifying conflict shadows the Third Age of Men, it has fallen into total disrepair and been transformed into a place of utter desolation; and its western side has become a frontier of war.

Eastern Osgiliath has fallen into the hands of the forces of Mordor: Orcs and Wargs and other fell creatures roam the ruins. But the western part of the city is patrolled by the Ithilien Rangers, Men of Gondor under the captaincy of Faramir, son of Denethor of Minas Tirith.

If the Enemy can overcome this last-ditch defense, Gondor lies at the mercy of Sauron's army, and the great city of Minas Tirith will be the only hope left to Men before the Shadow falls over all the Free Peoples of Middle-earth.

THE RETURN OF THE KING

"Gondor has no King . . ."

Although the Stewards and people of Gondor have lost faith in the possibility of the return of a king to rule their realm, a distant scion of the royal house still exists, one of the shadowy ancient people of the North, the Dúnedain. As a sign of his heritage he wears the Ring of Barahir, an heirloom of the house of Beren One-hand. He was known to the hobbits first as Strider; then in Rivendell was his true identity revealed: Aragorn, son of Arathorn, heir of Isildur of Gondor.

Many challenges has Aragorn had to meet and face on the long road to his return, and the sternest are yet to come. As the shadows deepen and need is greatest, the second token of his kingship shall be brought to him.

It is now time for Aragorn to reveal himself to the Dark Lord, through the palantír of Orthanc, the seeing-stone that Gandalf bears, for to know that the heir of Isildur lives and walks the earth will be a sore blow to Sauron's heart and may further distract his Great Eye away from the Ringbearer on his perilous trek toward the Mountain of Fire.

THE PALANTÍR

But instead Sauron offers Aragorn a terrible vision: of his beloved, pale and lifeless, reft of her Elven immortality. The Evenstar, the glittering jewel that Arwen gave to Aragorn as a token of their love, shatters. Far away across Middle-earth, the effect of this sorcery is felt: the power of the Evenstar is broken. But to embrace a life on Middle-earth and live as a mortal with her love was the choice that Arwen had already made. Even Sauron's malice cannot destroy their love.

THE SWORD REFORGED

From the shards of Isildur's ancient sword, Narsil, which cut from the Dark Lord's hand the One Ring in the great battle that ended the Second Age, and that has until now lain in Rivendell, has come the Sword Reforged — Andúril, Flame of the West! Made by the Elven-smiths, it bears seven stars, a crescent sun, and a rayed moon, and its blade is carved with runes.

"Sauron will not have forgotten the sword of Elendil . . . The blade that broke shall return to Minas Tirith"

THE PATHS OF THE DEAD

"Every path you have trod through wilderness, through war,

has led to this road. This is your test, Aragorn…"

In the Second Age of Middle-earth, the Men of the Mountains swore an oath to the last King of Gondor at the Black Stone of Erech that they would come to his aid to fight against the Dark Lord; but when his need was desperate, they fled away into the Haunted Mountain, the Dwimorberg. And so Isildur cursed them: that they should never rest in peace until they had fulfilled their oath. Now Aragorn, Isildur's heir, must call them to their oath, to aid the Free Peoples of Middle-earth in their dire struggle against the Shadow.

"The dead are following… I see shapes of men and of horses and pale banners

like shreds of clouds, and spears like winter thickets on a misty night"

The road to the Dimholt is ominously silent: in that haunted place nothing stirs, neither wind nor bird. At the root of the mountain gapes a dark door like the mouth of night. Signs and figures are carved above its wide arch, and fear flows from it like a gray vapor. No one living who has stepped through this door has returned alive; but Aragorn, Gimli, and Legolas enter with grim resolve. Ghastly, bony hands clutch at them out of the chill darkness; fog swirls; voices wail. All around them are the Dead: their King and row upon row of his spectral warriors. As they gather for attack, Aragorn draws the Sword Reforged and claims their allegiance anew, promising in exchange for their duty that he will release them from their living death. They listen; and they follow…

SAURON

The Dark Lord's history has long, deep roots. He entered the world as a Maia (as did the Istari wizards — Saruman and Gandalf — in a later age) under the direction of the Valar, those purest of spirits, and his task was to tend to the world's good. But Sauron fell under the influence of Morgoth, a Vala who had betrayed his fellows and embraced evil and the pursuit of dominion. Thus was Sauron seduced into his allegiance. As Morgoth's servant, he learned much of evil and power, and following the Great Battle that ended the First Age, in which Morgoth was at last cast down by the Valar, he fled to Middle-earth and there began his reign of terror.

He established himself in the dread realm of Mordor, east of the River Anduin and separated from Gondor, the nearest kingdom of Man, by the Mountains of Shadow. There he began the construction of a mighty tower from which he might look out over his own province and the world beyond, which he sought to ensnare. In the long centuries that followed, Sauron set himself to corrupting the races of Elves and Men and devising a plan by which he might bring dominion of all the Free Peoples of Middle-earth under his control. First, he labored with the Elven-smiths to create the Rings of Power: nine for the Kings of Men, seven for the Dwarves, and three for the Elves. But some time afterward he treacherously forged for himself a ruling ring in the heart of Orodruin, the Mountain of Fire; and sorcerously imbued it with a great deal of his magical power. But the Elves evaded his trap, and the Rings proved to have little effect on the Dwarves; the Men, however, proved weak and fell quickly under his influence.

Using the power of the One Ring, Sauron completed his great tower of Barad-dûr and drew his forces about him. When his treachery became

clear, war was inevitable. The Elves took arms against him and cast him down; but he was not completely defeated until the great Battle of Dagorlad, which ended the Second Age of Middle-earth, when Isildur, son of the fallen King Elendil, cut the One Ring from Sauron's hand. Reduced to a fiery spirit form, and a great, ever-seeking Lidless Eye, Sauron retreated and set himself to the task of rebuilding his forces: a matter that proved far more difficult without the One Ring that, until a hobbit called Bilbo Baggins came by it following an encounter with the creature Gollum, remained lost even to his searching Eye.

But in the Third Age, as his servants traveled far and wide across Middle-earth, word came to him that the Ring was in a small rural backwater known as the Shire. There he sent his Black Riders, the nine Nazgûl on swift black steeds, and the quarry was flushed out into the open. Many times have his servants come close to retrieving the One Ring; and now it is making its own way towards him, through the borders of his Shadow Land: he senses its presence, and the Ring answers. It travels with two hobbits and their guide, the slinking spy, Gollum, who once

escaped from the dungeons of the Dark Tower and must therefore know well the return route. What hope can they possibly have in the face of the odds that await them? Tens of thousands of Orcs, Uruk-hai, Trolls, Haradrim, Easterlings, Mûmakil, fell beasts, and the Nine Riders has he gathered about him for an army; to enter Mordor with the Dark Lord's most precious possession is surely to walk into his very arms, and the destruction of the free world.

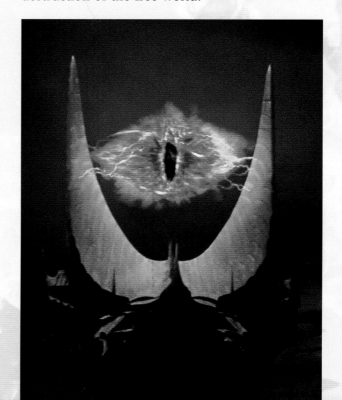

BARAD-DÛR

"Towers and battlements, tall as hills..."

Once he had forged the One Ring, Sauron used the power with which he had invested it to create the greatest fortress in Middle-earth, and he named it Barad-dûr: the Dark Tower. Here, at the south end of the Mountains of Ash, in the midst of the volcanic Gorgoroth Plain in the dread land of Mordor, he might dwell and further his treacherous plans for dominion. Fell runes and evil sigils denoting the sorcery with which it was made cover its towering black walls. It is a place of untold horror.

From the torture chambers in its dungeons, in which racks and wheels are manned by cruel Orcs, its fiery factories of war, its eyeless prisons and mighty courts, to the vast iron crown at its apex, Barad-dûr climbs thousands of feet into grim skies, as massive and forbidding as any mountain peak. And between the spiked iron pinnacles at the top of the tower, the Great Eye shimmers, constantly awake and aware, constantly seeking the Ring and the one who bears it.

NAZGÛL

"They once were Kings of Men…"

In the Second Age, Sauron ensnared nine Kings, proud rulers of the Men of Middle-earth, by giving each of them a Ring of Power and promising them long life and endless power. Thus, being Men and weak of will, they fell prey to his sorcery and were corrupted so that their mortal essence fell away and they became wraiths, destined to live in the world as undead creatures, bound always to his servitude.

They appear dressed all in flowing black robes and rusted mail, and carry long swords; where their faces should be is only darkness; but their true selves, which can be seen only by one wearing the Ring, is spectral and fearsome indeed. As writhing, tormented beings, all of tattered gray and white they are, their expressions distorted by the greed and grief of their condition, their crowns a mockery of the honor and rule they have lost.

The Nine are known also as Ringwraiths and as Black Riders when, mounted on vast black steeds, they searched far and wide through the Shire for the one called Baggins, who was rumored to have in his possession the Ruling Ring. As Frodo, bequeathed the Ring by his Uncle Bilbo, and his companions made their way from Bree to Rivendell, they encountered the Ringwraiths at Weathertop, where Frodo was stabbed with a sorcerous Morgul-blade, a terrible wound that would trouble him until the end of his days.

Their home is Minas Morgul, the Tower of Black Sorcery, where their shrieking cries pierce the night and strike chill fear into the hearts of any who hear them. Most terrifying of the Dark

Lord's servants, no man can kill them; although, perhaps because of some vestige of their once-mortal selves, they are afraid of fire.

FELL BEASTS

Having lost their steeds in the floods of Bruinen below Rivendell, the Nine Riders have come by more terrible mounts by far. As Sam, Frodo, and Gollum cross the Dead Marshes, a huge winged shape swoops overhead, gliding soundlessly across the wide mere. This new horror is a fell beast out of Mordor — a huge, black, naked thing, its vast, leathery wings stretched between the wide span of its bony fingers like the wings of some monstrous bat.

It is a creature of an older world, one of those that bred in cold mountain eyries and were taken and nurtured on nameless foods by the Dark Lord until they grew larger than any other flying thing.

Mounted on such a creature, the Nazgûl can travel at great speed and oversee every part of Sauron's realm. Nothing can hide from them…

THE WITCH-KING OF ANGMAR

"The most fell of all his captains…"

The Lord of the Ringwraiths, and the mightiest servant of the Dark Lord, is the Witch-king of Angmar. Greater than the other Nazgûl, he dresses all in sable, save for a silver helm that flickers with perilous light.

Of his origins, little is known except that he was once a king and a sorcerer, but he was ensnared by Sauron when he received the greatest of the Nine Rings. After Sauron's fall in the Battle of Dagorlad at the end of the Second Age of Middle-earth, he fled into the shadows and thence to the lands between the Ettenmoors and the Northern Waste, where he created for himself the realm of Angmar, and there became known as the Witch-king of Angmar.

In later times he and the rest of the Nine Riders took control of Minas Ithil and renamed it Minas Morgul, Tower of Black Sorcery, and there he remained until called upon by his lord, who in the Third Age had regained some of his former power. Sent out to regain the One Ring from the hobbit "Baggins," he struck down Frodo at Weathertop, dealing him a terrible wound with his sorcerous blade.

"His own folk quail at him, and they would slay themselves at his bidding…"

As the commander of Sauron's dark forces, it is the Witch-king who, clad in black armor and helm and armed with sword and flail, leads the great host out of the gates of Minas Morgul at his master's bidding, over the bridge and away west to war in Gondor, to lay siege to the fair city of Minas Tirith, where, against all likelihood and prophecy, he will meet his doom.

HARADRIM

"Very cruel wicked Men…Almost as bad as Orcs…"

From the South comes a fierce race of Men, inhabitants of a realm of Harad. For millennia they have warred with Gondor, even when defeated remaining a threat on the kingdom's borders. Tall and dark and cruel, they are fearsome warriors, especially when armed with their wickedly sharp spears.

MÛMAKIL

"Gray as a mouse,

Big as a house…"

Their greatest advantage in war is the use of mûmakil (in singular, mûmak) — known also by the hobbits as Oliphaunts — which bear great war-towers packed with Haradrim archers into the midst of battle, trampling and crushing their enemies, men and horses alike, under their massive feet, their spiked tusks swaying perilously, impaling those in their way.

In the Battle of the Pelennor Fields, in the fields outside Minas Tirith, these fierce warriors and their fighting mûmakil will be deadly foes to face for the soldiery of Gondor and the Riders of Rohan.

THE CORSAIRS OF UMBAR

A fleet of black-sailed pirate ships, rowed by slaves and crewed by the notoriously black-hearted Corsairs of Umbar, comes from the south to ally itself with the forces of Sauron. The fleet sails up the River Anduin toward Minas Tirith, leaving ruin and murder in its wake. If the Corsairs reach Gondor's first city, the forces of darkness are sure to overwhelm the defenders, for Minas Tirith cannot fight a battle on all fronts, and its docks are vulnerable. But Gondor's armies and allies are already in desperate straits.

With the foresight and command that mark his heritage as the true King of Men, Aragorn, son of Arathorn, quickly apprehends the danger. Leading the Army of the Dead — a rolling wave of ghosts who carry everything before them — Aragorn does battle with the Corsairs before they can join the rest of Sauron's forces. And when this latest threat has been met and annihilated, the five thousand specters are free to turn their attention to the field of battle. Orcs will flee in their thousands, terrified mûmakil trampling them down in their panic; trolls will fall, just when it seemed all was lost. The Army of the Dead will swarm up the sides of the war towers and kill the Haradrim soldiery within, then rout the Orcs until the Pelennor Fields lie silent and strewn with dead. And then they will enter Minas Tirith itself, and scour from Gondor's city every last trace of darkness.

ENGINES OF WAR

The forces that the Dark Lord has amassed and that will now bear down upon Gondor are vast and terrifying: endless columns of Orcs and Uruk-hai, trolls and unnamed monsters; an army of Haradrim and their massive, fighting mûmakil fitted out with great war-towers manned with archers; and above them all the Nine Riders swoop and dive, mounted on their vile fell beasts. It is an army to drive a chill into the heart of the surviving Men of Gondor, now gathered inside the mighty fortress city of Minas Tirith.

The city is said to be impregnable; but so it was believed of the ancient stronghold of Helm's Deep, which nevertheless was breached by Saruman's army of Uruk-hai with their ballistas and ladders and their great battering ram, which broke down Helm's Gate. Had it not been then for the arrival of the Rohirrim and Gandalf the White, Helm's Deep would surely have fallen and all its defenders and the refugees hiding in the Glittering Caves beneath its foundations would have been slaughtered.

Sauron's forces are bringing their own engines of war to this new battlefield, but they are greater by far — both in size and effectiveness — than those that were manufactured in Saruman's factories of Isengard. From the vast pits beneath Barad-dûr, from its furnaces and foundries, and from the smithies of East Osgiliath, will come new horrors: siege towers of gigantic size hauled by armored mountain-trolls and manned by hordes of Orcs, wherein the invaders can take safe cover as the towers are wheeled up to the walls of the city; massive catapults that can bear pitch and fire and stones.

And last of all will come a mighty battering ram, greater by far than that which broke Helm's Gate; for the Gate of Gondor is strongly made indeed, wrought of steel and iron, and guarded with towers and bastions of stone: yet it is the weakest point in the city's defenses. Grond is the name of this great engine of war, after the mace of the first Dark Lord, Morgoth, who once was Sauron's master; and it has been long in the making in Mordor. At over a hundred feet in length, it is as long as a forest tree and it swings on huge iron chains. Its head is fashioned of black steel in the likeness of a ravening wolf, and fire shoots from its eyes. Four great beasts draw it, bull-headed and massive of body: terrors in themselves, for their like have never before been seen on Middle-earth. Mountain-trolls will wield it and Orcs will defend it; and the Witch-king of Angmar will direct its use.

HOBBITS AS HEROES

"The stars are veiled . . . a storm is coming"

A great cloud hangs over all the land between Rohan and the Mountains of Shadow, and it is deepening. War has already begun. In such grim times, all must play their part, even folk as small as hobbits. Now it is the turn of Meriadoc Brandybuck and Peregrin Took — Merry and Pippin — to prove their true worth: for the first time in their lives, they must take separate paths and follow new masters, for Gandalf has removed Pippin to Minas Tirith for his own protection, after the young hobbit stole a look in the seeing-stone of Orthanc and thus attracted the attention of the Great Eye.

At only twenty-nine years of age — still four years short of his coming-of-age in Shire reckoning — Pippin is indeed very young; the youngest of the four companions who set out from Hobbiton. In Minas Tirith he is presented to Denethor, the Steward of Gondor, father to the man who fell trying to protect him and Merry from Saruman's Uruk-hai at Amon Hen. In a gesture of thanks for Boromir's sacrifice, Pippin offers his service to Denethor, and is duly fitted out in the uniform of the Tower Guard, a great honor indeed.

Arrayed all in black and silver, he wears a hauberk of forged steel and a high silver helmet

with small raven wings on either side, set with a silver star in the center of the circlet. Above the mail he wears a short surcoat of black, and embroidered on the breast in silver is the White Tree of Gondor. It is the livery once worn by Faramir, Boromir's brother, when he was a child; and while his heart and will may be as strong as any grown man's, Pippin is still mistaken for a child as he walks the streets of Gondor's great city. But his first task in this uniform — though it is not a task entrusted by his new master — is to light the warning beacons at the summit of Mount Mindolluin and thus to summon aid; as in answer, the lights of the subsequent beacons can be seen over the White Mountains as far as Edoras.

"Here do I swear fealty and service to Gondor, in peace or war, in living or dying, from this hour henceforth, until my lord release me, or death take me"

Meanwhile, Merry finds himself amongst the Horse-lords of the Riddermark with King Théoden of Rohan, as the light of the warning beacon is seen and the King summons all able-bodied men to muster at Dunharrow for the long ride to Minas Tirith. Determined to play his part in the war, Merry bravely offers the service of his sword to Théoden, who receives the offer graciously, deeming that Merry shall henceforth be an Esquire of Rohan; and so he, like Pippin, is fitted out in the war-accouterments of his new master: the finely tooled leather armor of the Rohirrim, a helm and cloak.

"He knows not to what end he rides, yet if he knew he would still go on"

But at Dunharrow, great disappointment awaits him: the King releases him from his service and will take him no further, for it is from there three days' hard riding to the beleaguered city, and the horses of the Rohirrim are too large and too strong for one as small as a hobbit to manage on their own: he would only be a burden.

Resigned to his fate, Merry turns away, only to be swept up by an anonymous Rider and borne away to war.

THE SIEGE OF GONDOR

"Courage will now be your best defense against the storm that is at hand"

Outside the walls of Minas Tirith, Gondor's greatest city, Orcish armies mass, thousands upon thousands of them with their engines of war, each of them bearing flaming torches and an unquenchable hatred for their enemy. Above them swoop the Nazgûl, striking fear into their own troops as into the hearts of the defenders of Minas Tirith. The Army of Darkness hugely outnumbers the soldiery within; and with the reports of a great fleet of corsairs sailing north from the hostile city of Umbar, and the whereabouts of the Ringbearer unknown, the future looks grim indeed for the Free Peoples of Middle-earth.

But now Gandalf is conducting the defense of Minas Tirith; and he is indomitable. He commands that the defenders return to their stations, lined up along the battlements of the lower levels as they watch the Orc army, tens of thousands strong, come within range of the outer wall. The Orcish catapults throw down the gauntlet with an opening salvo, but instead of the usual shot or flaming ballast it is with a new atrocity that they assault the Men of Gondor. With their siege towers, Sauron's army may make incursions into the lower levels of Minas Tirith; with burning pitch they may set fire to its ancient stonework; but terror is a far worse enemy than flame. In despair and fury, the Gondorians fire their great trebuchets out at the marauding Orcs, sending boulders raining down upon them, and archers loose their arrows from all seven levels of Minas Tirith's battlements.

Orcish archers return fire, and soon the air is black with the exchange of deadly missiles. Each side suffers under the devastating onslaught. Then siege towers are brought up to the walls of the city and a battering ram thuds into its gates, but to no avail. Until, that is, eight mountain-trolls and four great, bull-headed monsters draw in the massive wheeled battering ram, Grond.

Nothing could possibly withstand the onslaught of such an engine: even the steel- and iron-bound gates of Minas Tirith are no match for the tempered steel and black sorcery of its evil wolf-head. It smashes the Gate of Gondor, and Orcs spill into the First Circle of the city,

beneath the archway where no enemy has ever passed.

Gandalf leads a counterattack with Gondorian soldiers and there ensues fierce hand-to-hand fighting. All around, buildings are aflame. Fires rage unchecked in the First Circle: it is time to retreat to Second; and soon after that to the Third.

As the Lord of the Nazgûl, the Witch-king of Angmar, and his fell beast loom over Gandalf and Shadowfax in the Fourth Circle of the city, all hope seems to be lost.

But from the distance comes the faint ring of war-horns. Rohan has come!

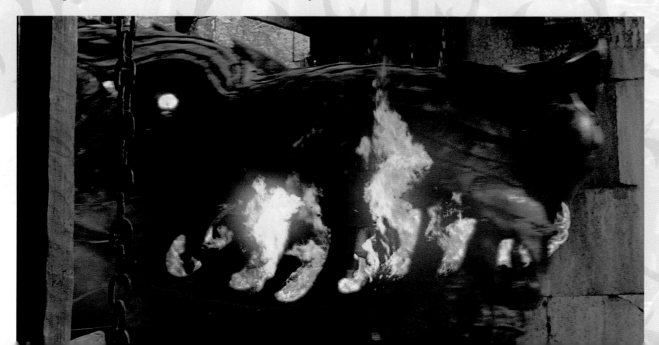

THE BATTLE OF THE PELENNOR FIELDS

"Say to Denethor that in this hour the King of the Mark himself will come down to the land of Gondor, though may be he will not ride back"

Horns sound like a storm upon the plain and a thunder in the mountains: the Rohirrim have come to give aid to their old ally in this darkest of times. Théoden and Éomer ride together, uncle and nephew reunited at last, arrayed in the magnificent leather armor and the crested helmets of their people. The white horsetail plume on Éomer's helm floats in his speed; King Théoden gallops upon Snowmane, and his banner is a white horse upon a field of green. Their arrival is a glorious sight; a sight to set hope in the hearts of those who defend Minas Tirith, and to strike fear into the enemy.

From Dunharrow, the muster has brought six thousand spears; and though that is far less than King Théoden had hoped for, it is a warlike and fearsome army, for the Rohirrim are tough and

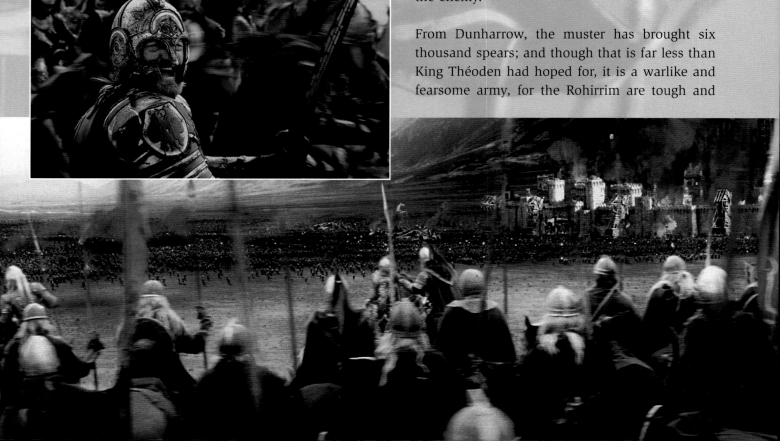

grim and well-versed in the skills of war; and they have seen how with fire and sword the Shadow has already fallen upon their own people: they have scores to settle.

The Witch-king screeches and his mount rises into the air with a great flap of its wings as the six thousand Rohan horsemen step up onto the skyline.

Now ensues the greatest battle of the War of the Ring between the armies of Sauron — including Haradrim, Easterlings, Orcs, and mûmakil — led by the Lord of the Nazgûl; and the forces of Minas Tirith, all those that could be mustered from the surrounding lands, joined by the forces of Osgiliath and Ithilien and the Riders of Rohan.

HEROIC DEEDS

"Ride now, ride now, ride to ruin and the world's ending!"

As the front of the first rank of the Rohirrim gallops into battle like a breaker crashing to the shore, the battle-fury of their forefathers runs through King Théoden and his men. War-horns blast out; sunlight gleams off helm and weaponry. Nothing can withstand that first charge. An entire company of Orcs vanishes beneath trampling hooves. But having overcome the first wave of Orcs, there are ever more, and then Haradrim and mûmakil, bearing huge war-towers packed with Haradrim archers, which bellow as they are driven mercilessly to war by their Harad masters. They lumber into the sea of men, trampling and crushing riders and horses beneath their vast feet, impaling the hapless upon their spiked tusks, as rains of Harad arrows fall all around.

Then it is that the Lord of the Nazgûl, the Witch-king of Angmar, swoops down and his fell beast grabs up in its cruel claws both Théoden and his white stallion, Snowmane; and thus comes the death of the valiant King of Rohan.

"Do not come between the

Nazgûl and his prey!"

Then an unnamed Rider steps into the breach and with a single sweep of his shining sword beheads the vile monster on which the Witch-king is mounted. It is an act of extraordinary courage: for surely none can withstand the Lord of the Nazgûl; indeed, ancient prophecy has foretold such, deeming that no living man can kill him. Yet the Witch-king of Angmar's antagonist is no mere man, but Éowyn: valorous shieldmaiden of Rohan and niece of the fallen king, who has ridden from Dunharrow in disguise, driven by her desire for battle and her love for the Lord Aragorn. Now she — and the hobbit whom she has borne all the way from the Muster — will try to avenge King Théoden's death, or they will die in the attempt.

THE BLACK GATE

Once the Battle of the Pelennor Fields is won — more by the dead than the living — all that is left for Aragorn and his allies to aid the quest to destroy the Ring is to confront the Dark Lord in his own realm, and thus draw his attention away from Sam and Frodo as they make their lonely, desperate way into the Land of Shadow.

After the slaughter on the Pelennor Fields, their numbers are perilously few: they stand no chance of victory against the mighty army that Sauron still maintains within the Black Gate, the great iron rampart across the haunted pass into Mordor at the meeting of the Ephel Dúath (The Mountains of Shadow) and the Ered Lithui (the Ashen Mountains).

"What did they bring, the Kings of old?

From over the sundered seas?

Seven stars, and seven stones

And one white tree…"

Wearing the armor of his forebears, with the White Tree of Gondor on his chest, and bearing the Sword Reforged, Aragorn, once known as Strider, leads the remainder of the Nine Companions and the Captains of the West to what must surely be their deaths…

THE LIEUTENANT OF THE TOWER

"His name is remembered in no tale…"

At the Gate they cry out a challenge; a challenge which will be answered by one of the Dark Lord's chief servants. The apparition who rides out to meet them is the Lieutenant of the Dark Tower of Barad-dûr, a creature of sorcery now grown advanced in evil and cruel cunning. For so long has he served his master that he no longer bears his own name, but is known merely as the Mouth of Sauron. He rides a huge and hideous black horse with a face like a frightful mask, more like a skull than a living head, and eyes of flame; and his own visage is hardly more fair.

Gleeful and arrogant, the Mouth of Sauron delivers to the brave visitors the false tidings that the Ringbearer has been apprehended by the Orcs of Cirith Ungol and taken to the torture chambers of the Dark Tower. In evidence of this, he flourishes the mithril shirt taken from Frodo, and a great despair engulfs them.

Moments later, drums beat out and fires flare up. The Black Gate of Mordor swings open, and a vast army of Orcs marches out.

"There may come a day when the courage of Men fails…an hour of wolves before the Age of Men comes crashing down – but it will not be this day! This day we fight!"

THE TREACHERY OF GOLLUM

"We hates them, nassty hobbitses…"

As Sam and Frodo make their slow, painful, perilous journey across the forsaken places of Middle-earth on their quest to destroy the One Ring in the fires of Mount Doom — the one place in the world where it can be unmade — they are accompanied by one who claims to be able to aid their safe passage into Mordor.

Gollum — who used to be called Sméagol, a creature much like a hobbit — has a long and strange history: for he too was a Ringbearer, of sorts, for many, many years. Having murdered his cousin Déagol to acquire the golden trinket they found while out fishing, Sméagol fell under the malevolent influence of the Ring and wandered away from his homeland to take refuge from the light in the caves beneath the Misty Mountains. And it was there where he finally lost his "Precious" to Frodo's uncle, Bilbo Baggins.

"Master carries heavy burden…Smeagol knows: Smeagol carried burden many years"

Now, the two parts of him — Sméagol, who still vaguely remembers the time when he was not the slave of the Ring and is able to experience feelings that have not been entirely warped and wicked; and Gollum, whose only wish is to take back the Ring for himself and see the thieves who carry it now dead and rotting — are warring for dominance of his soul. Shall he lead the hobbits, as he has promised, via safe ways into the Land of Shadow; or shall he lead them to destruction and then reunite himself with the Precious?

"Treachery, treachery I fear; treachery of

that miserable creature!"

Frodo's apparent treachery in allowing Faramir and his rangers to take Gollum prisoner in Ithilien has weighted the scales: now the personality of Sméagol has been subsumed by the ravening greed of Gollum. He cannot kill the two hobbits himself: no, for the Fat One is strong and bears a dreaded Elven rope that chokes and burns.

But if he cannot do the deed himself, he knows one who can. So it is through Morgul Vale and up the Stair of Cirith Ungol that Gollum leads the hobbits. It is not a way they would have chosen, had they known what lay ahead...

MINAS MORGUL

"That accursed valley passed into evil
a very long time ago"

Minas Ithil — the Tower of the Moon — was once the fortress-city of Isildur, son of Elendil. It was built high in an upland valley beneath the Mountains of Shadow, on the road that runs south out of the fair lands of Ithilien, and in its day it was a city both beautiful and bright, and the Moon lit its inner courts with a wondrous silver light.

But in the early part of the Third Age, the Tower of the Moon was lost to Sauron's forces and became the lair of the Nazgûl, the Nine Ringwraiths; and then it became known as Minas Morgul, the Tower of Black Sorcery. Now it has the radiance of corpse-light: a faint, ailing, noisome green, and in its walls and towers windows show like countless holes all looking inward, to emptiness and ruin.

"Ruined city, yes, very nasty place,
full of enemies"

A road leads out of the dead city, crossing a bridge adorned with the carved forms of people and beasts, all of them loathsome and corrupt. Beneath the bridge, the water steams with vile and poisonous fumes; and all about the meads on either side of the stream luminous white flowers glow with an eerie, charnel beauty. It is a grim and unnerving place, even without the shrieking presence of the Nazgûl; or the vast army of Orcs that issues from its cavernous doors...

THE PASS OF CIRITH UNGOL

A near-vertical stairway has been cut into the sheer rock that leads upward from the gate of Minas Morgul into the dizzying heights above and up to the only pass that leads through the Mountains of Shadow. The pass is guarded by the Tower of Cirith Ungol, and the way is perilous; not only because the stairs are treacherous and the tower manned by vicious Orcs — but also for the unseen horror that gives both pass and tower their name, did the hobbits but know it.

Up the stairs Gollum leads Frodo and Sam. The steps are worn and smooth, narrow and unevenly spaced. Some are already broken, or crack if a foot is set upon them. They are so great and so steep that the hobbits — smaller creatures than this stairway was first made for — climb them as if climbing an endless ladder, a ladder that stretches for two thousand feet from the valley floor into the mists above.

It is hard not to look down, hard to ignore the chill void at their heels that beckons every misstep; but still Gollum clambers upward, and all they can do is follow.

At the top of the ridge lies the Tower of Cirith Ungol: a great three-tiered watch-tower and fortress now garrisoned by Orcs from both Barad-dûr and Minas Morgul. As the hobbits climb,

they can see the Tower silhouetted in the cleft
between the mountains, guarding the way both
in and out of Mordor; beyond it, far out on the
Plain of Gorgoroth, lies Barad-dûr, with its iron
crown and Lidless Eye. The dull, red light that
can be spied through the cleft comes from
Orodruin — the Mountain of Fire; Mount Doom
itself — as great gouts of volcanic flame erupt
from its peak.

But the way is guarded not only by Orcs, but also
by the Two Watchers: two sentient statues of stone
emanating great evil. Each of the statues boasts
three vulture-heads, and each head faces inward,
outward, and across the gateway, ready to sound
an alarm if any intruder or spy should pass.

SHELOB

"Let her deal with them . . . she must eat. All she gets is filthy orcses.

She hungers for sweeter meats"

At the top of the stair at Cirith Ungol there lies a ravine through tall gray weathered rock. Gollum insists that the tunnels that lie within this ravine represent the only safe way through to the other side of the mountains, for the Pass is too vigilantly guarded — by the Two Watchers and the Orc garrison — for them to take that route. The mouth of this cavern emits a foul stench. Inside is utmost darkness.

Through an upward-leading tunnel they go, passing tributary passages that they sense rather than see in this lightless place. There is nothing in here but an ominous silence, yet Frodo senses some lurking malice; and, oddly, the walls are sticky to the touch.

"There's something worse than Gollum about. I can feel something looking at us"

As they penetrate deeper into the dark tunnels, there comes a venomous hissing sound; and Gollum flees, deserting the hobbit he had promised to guide safely through the mountains to Mordor. A pale green light begins to illuminate the tunnel. Now the true depth of Gollum's treachery is revealed. For the cavern into which he has led him is the lair of a vile and ancient horror...

"Long had she been hungry,
lurking in her den"

Shelob, the occupant of this rank catacomb, has dwelt here for millennia, before even Sauron came to Middle-earth, weaving webs of shadow in which to trap her prey and gorging herself on unwitting travelers — on Elves and Men who happened in her way; then on beasts that knew no better than to avoid her lair. In all this agelong time she has grown vast and bloated and bitter; but since the city below the Pass fell into ruin and became the haunt of the Nazgûl, her prey has also waned: now all she feeds upon is the odd unwary Orc.

Gollum happened upon this horror during his escape from Sauron's torture chambers, many years ago; ever since, she has lurked in his mind. Now, his plan to regain the One Ring may be fulfilled, for Shelob has no appetite for gold or power, only for flesh. Once she has trapped Frodo and eaten his poor body, the Ring will fall unregarded to the ground. And then Gollum may be reunited with his Precious…

THE COURAGE OF SAMWISE GAMGEE

"No onslaught more fierce was ever seen in the savage world of beasts…"

Samwise Gamgee is a gardener, and the son of a gardener. Before this long and arduous journey, he had never even left the Shire, let alone wielded a sword or faced an enemy. But his love and loyalty for his master, Frodo Baggins, has brought him a very long way from the lush pastures and comfortable inns of his home.

Sam would never have considered himself brave, or any sort of hero. He was always quite content with his lot; could not even raise the nerve to ask lovely Rosie Cotton for a dance. But now he has

stayed with the Elves in Rivendell and Lothlórien, traveled through the legendary Mines of Moria, traversed meres and mountains, seen Oliphaunts and ruined cities, fought Black Riders and Cave Trolls, Orcs and Uruk-hai.

But in all those matters he had little or no choice: his duty was to Frodo, and he followed blindly. Even facing the most appalling monster he has

encountered so far — with her many knobbed and steely legs; her vile clusters of eyes and wicked mandibles; her vast, bloated body and venomous claws — is not his greatest test; for the rage that surges up inside him when he sees what she has done to his beloved Frodo overtakes all reason. No, the most severe test of his extraordinary courage has yet to come.

"I have something to do before the end.

I must see it through…"

When he thinks his master dead and that all is lost, nothing would be so easy as to give up, to succumb to despair: to flee that awful place and somehow make his way back to the Shire, alone and grieving. But the Great Task still remains; and if Sam will not carry it through, there is no one left alive who can.

It is a brave decision, to take the Ring; and in doing so, Sam saves the entire quest. If he had not, the Orcs would have scavenged it from Frodo's body and taken it to Sauron, and shadow would have fallen over all the world. He may berate himself for believing his master dead — amidst all the horror and the carnage — when he is merely poisoned and paralyzed; but this error, and his courage, have turned back a tide of evil.

AMONG THE ORCS

In the midst of hostile territory, surrounded by thousands of Orcs and with the Lidless Eye searching constantly for the hobbit who bears the One Ring, Frodo and Sam are faced by a dilemma as they make their escape from the Tower of Cirith Ungol and their entry into the Land of Shadow, for Frodo's garments and belongings have been appropriated and squabbled over by the Tower Guards, and Sam has only his cloak to spare. But some of the Orcs who garrisoned the Tower are very little taller than the two hobbits, and so, although they may be disgusted by the rank stench of the enemy soldiers and appalled at having to scavenge raiment from the dead, Orc-armour and breeches it must be if they are to enter Mordor. Besides, the bizarre helmets will shield the faces of folk who look very little like the denizens of that grim place. It is a very effective disguise: too effective, maybe.

As the hobbits struggle across the foothills, they find themselves face to face with a large battalion of Orcs and are whipped into line by the overseer of that troop, and after a painful forced march soon find themselves in the midst of a vast Orc-army — hundreds of thousands of enemy soldiers encamped on the Gorgoroth Plain, ready to annihilate the remnants of the armies of Gondor and Rohan under Aragorn's command. Drums beat and torches flare in the night. Unspeakable things roast over campfires. All of Middle-earth will soon look like this — blighted and abused — unless Frodo's quest succeeds.

Orodruin, the Mountain of Fire — the final destination for the destruction of the One Ring — is clearly visible now through the brooding, ash-laden skies…

MOUNT DOOM

"There is no veil between me and the wheel of fire. I see it even with my waking eyes…"

Far across the Gorgoroth Plain, that giant volcano — Orodruin, the Mountain of Fire — is erupting. It casts great streams of ash and lava high into the air, illuminating the thick cloud that hangs over Mordor with a flickering, fiery orange light.

The closer Sam and Frodo approach, dragging their desperate, weary feet ever onward, the more violent and hellish their surroundings become: red heat hisses out of fissures, everywhere the rocks are jagged and razor-sharp, choking volcanic ash blankets the land, terrifying red lightning forks across the sky.

With the Ring burdening him ever more cruelly, by the time they reach the foot of the mountain, Frodo will be reduced to crawling on his hands and knees. Thousands of feet above them the volcano towers, its summit wreathed in fiery cloud. Even for two strong, able-bodied Men, the climb would be a feat. For two exhausted and traumatized hobbits at the very end of their resources — both physical and mental — it represents what appears an impossible task. Far, far above is the stone doorway of the Sammath Naur, which leads into the Crack of Doom — that great, lava-filled chasm in which Sauron first forged the One Ring, and the only place in all the world where it, and all its evil, can be unmade. Yet all this remains shrouded to them; as does the third creature that toils up this grim and vertiginous slope...

For these Shire folk, used to the soft greens and blues of a gentle, rainwashed rural landscape, with its rolling pastures and flower-filled meadows, its millponds and woodlands, it must look like the very end of the world.

"Wicked Baggins!
Mustn't go that way, mustn't hurt Precious!"

FRODO'S CHOICE

"Destroy it now…throw it into the fire!"

Never has any mortal in possession of a Ring of Power relinquished it willingly. Even the lesser Rings have claimed the essence of their wearers, reducing them to monstrous wraiths, incorporeal in the world they wished to rule, their souls bound to the service of the Dark Lord, who seduced them with lies and then enslaved them.

But the One Ring — the Ring that rules all other Rings of Power — has an evil force all its own, and contains a large part of Sauron's dark magic. Isildur, son of Elendil, King of Gondor, struck the One Ring from Sauron's hand and cast him down in the battle that ended the Second Age of Middle-earth; but when he climbed Mount Doom to destroy the artifact as urged by Lord Elrond of the Elves, his will failed him, and he kept the Ring, to his own undoing; a failure that led to the fall of his line and, hundreds of years later, to the War of the Ring.

Bilbo Baggins found it most difficult and painful to lose the Ring, and aged as soon as it left him. Gandalf felt its presence and — for all his might and lore — dared not touch the One Ring for fear of the corruption it might work upon him. Galadriel, the Lady of the Golden Wood, who already held Nenya, one of the three Rings forged

But of all things, it is the creature once called Sméagol who best knows the seductive power of the One Ring. Warped by the proximity of his "Precious," "Sméagol" has been subsumed by "Gollum," who has forgotten all that was ever good or gentle in his being: the loss of the Ring has caused him such intense pain and avarice that he is determined to regain it, no matter what the price.

Frodo must enter the chambers of the Sammath Naur and cast the One Ring into the boiling lava of the Crack of Doom, the fissure that lies far below. In doing so, he must relinquish the vast potential of the Ruling Ring, all its seductive power and might. It will require immense strength of will to carry his great quest through to the end.

"I have made my choice…"

for the Elves, had the chance to take the Ruling Ring from Frodo in Lothlórien, but would not accept it for knowledge that it would render her most terrible. Boromir fell beneath its spell, and would have taken it as his own; his brother Faramir proved stronger; but their father, Denethor, craved the power it represents.

THE CROWNING OF KING ELESSAR

"Now come the days of the King, and may they be blessed

while the thrones of the Valar endure"

With Sauron defeated and the Dark Tower destroyed, the Shadow's armies dispersed and bewildered, and the Ringwraiths fallen screaming from the skies, the Third Age of Middle-earth has come to an end as the Second Age did so many centuries before. But this time Sauron has been utterly defeated, the greater part of his sorcery unmade in the Crack of Doom.

And now it is the time for Men to step to the fore and guide the future of Middle-earth. The King has returned. Men have had no king for millennia; but Aragorn, son of Arathorn, the heir of Isildur, has reunited the Free Peoples of Middle-earth against the Shadow and earned his crown.

In Minas Tirith, in a blizzard of white petals, with the city gleaming in the bright sun, the Crown of Gondor will be placed on Aragorn's head by Gandalf the White and thus he shall be crowned King Elessar. And Arwen, daughter of Elrond, princess of the Elves, who turned her back on the immortal life of her people for the love of this mortal man, shall the King take to wife.

Éomer, son of Éomund, nephew of Théoden, shall be crowned King of Rohan, and Faramir, son of Denethor, shall be honored as Prince of Ithilien and marry the Lady Éowyn of Rohan. And thus begins the Fourth Age of Middle-earth.

THE BREAKING OF THE FELLOWSHIP

And so the Fellowship of the Ring, the Nine Companions who came together in Rivendell so long ago, who set out largely in ignorance of the vast and terrifying events that lay before them, has fulfilled its purpose. The Ring is destroyed, Middle-earth is saved, and one of their number — Aragorn, son of Arathorn — revealed as the King of Men, has been restored to his rightful throne.

Now the Fellowship must disband.

Legolas faces a hard choice: to leave with his own kind for immortal life in the Undying Lands, or to remain behind in the world of Men. In the end, he decides to stay in Middle-earth and to dwell in the fair woods of Ithilien.

Gimli will become Lord of the Glittering Caves of Aglarond that lie beneath Helm's Deep; and for his close companionship with Legolas, he will earn the name of Elf-friend.

Merry has been made a Captain of the Mark of Rohan and Pippin a Knight of Gondor; with Frodo and Sam they will return as conquering heroes to Hobbiton, and there, in times to come, Sam will be elected Mayor of Hobbiton. And, although it took all of his courage, he finally asked for the hand of the lovely Rosie Cotton. It was the bravest thing he ever did.

THE GREY HAVENS

"I Aear cân ven na mar"
The Sea calls us home

But Frodo cannot stay in Hobbiton. He has endured too much, and something in him has been worn down by his experiences. With Bilbo — now extremely old and frail — and Gandalf the White, whose task is over, he will leave on the ship departing for Valinor, for the Undying Lands. It is the last sailing of the Elves.

"I think I'm ready for another adventure…"

In the beautiful gardens of the Grey Havens — the home of Círdan the ship-maker, Lord of Elves — Frodo will make his sorrowful farewells to those who will stay behind, before boarding the graceful white swan ship that lies at the dock and that will bear him away from the world of mortals forever.

"And though I oft have passed them by,

A day will come at last when I

Shall take the hidden paths that run

West of the Moon, East of the Sun."